Travails of Death

A Novella

By

James Lynch

2025

Table of Contents

Chapter One: Lucy

The morning of Monday September fourth 2016 was bright and sunny. It was a beautiful and warm late Summer's day, as Lucy Albright walked slowly that day the short distance from home to her new Secondary College. Her fair hair was proudly cut, but not too short. It had been especially washed and styled by her Gran for the occasion.

So, proudly sporting her new school uniform, fiddling with the waist-band her new school skirt and tucking it to lift the level of the skirt slightly above her knees, she walked smartly to her new secondary school, the Kelvin Secondary Technical College.

Earlier during the last school year in primary school, she had celebrated her twelfth birthday and was scheduled to move from the primary school to the nearby Kelvin Secondary Technical College beginning this very day. There had been a crush of parents seeking a place in that particular College for their child. It was a successful secondary level educational institution and competition for a place was hot. It thus had a very good reputation, although Lucy's teachers had needed to quote her 'weak' family background as a reason to obtain a place for her.

Lucy was excited yet also a little apprehensive. She was excited that she had obtained a place at the secondary technical school of her Gran's choice so near to her home, which not by any means all of her primary class had been able to accomplish. But, on the other hand, she was apprehensive about the new friends that she would have to make and what would be expected of her at her new school.

True one or maybe two of the group of her friends from the primary school would likely be at the new College too. But most of her clique had either been allocated to a different secondary school or they had been sent to private schools by their parents.

Nervously she fingered her new smart-phone calling round her circle of friends and trying to find out which friends she would be seeing that day. Her father had sent the phone to her with his birthday wishes on a lovely card, although he did not come to see her. In fact, he rarely did now. Her father and her mother lived separately, as he was now living with another woman some distance away and his mother was likewise living some distance from Lucy's house with her most recent boyfriend.

But Lucy still lived in the same large 1930s Council house in the English Midlands town where she and her mother and father had originally lived immediately after Lucy' birth. She only rarely saw her father and then only fleetingly on the rare occasion when he visited her mother to sort out the financial and other difficulties between her two parents caused by their legal separation.

Mawkishly, she was carrying her father's birthday card with her today in her rucksack and holding her smart-phone to her ear, making enquiries from her friends about their allocated school locations.

The very fact of taking her phone to school with her was in spite of the fact that her Gran had received a circular from the new school, stating the terms of studentship and particularly that smartphones should not be brought into school.

The letter did, however, offer a safe haven for students' phones from their entry to school in the morning until home-time in the afternoon in the provision of lockable boxes, just in case they had inadvertently forgotten the recommendation, which of course Lucy had! The letter pointed out that it was a serious infringement of school rules to use such a phone on the school premises and there could be serious consequences, sanctions indeed for any infringements.

The letter also emphasised the need for courtesy to staff and other students at all times, homework discipline for children and parents, a stipulation that drugs, vapes and knives of any kind were not permitted in College or its environs and the letter concluded with a strong statement that these stipulations would be strictly enforced.

The circular letter also informed Lucy's mother that her daughter would be in Miss Moverley's Standard One class for the first year. Lucy was pleased about this as all her teachers in the primary school had been women and she got on well with all of them. The letter also stated that there would be a meeting for parents early in the next term, so that they could acquaint themselves with the College and its regulations and meet their child's teacher to discuss their child's progress.

Lucy had done well at her primary school, which she had attended since entering the reception class at the age of four. In spite of her mother's extremely rare attendances at parents' evenings, Lucy had a sharp mind and had used her intelligence well, particularly in English language and mathematics, but also in history and general sciences.

As she rose up the class groups of succeeding years, she had been popular with each of the teachers, always willing to raise questions about what the students were learning and to volunteer for tasks such as collecting the text-books and educational materials or filling the decreasingly used inkpots.

In the final class she had been offered one of the few sought-after roles of ink and paint monitor by Miss Benson, to whom she felt she had a particular attachment. It was she who had assisted Lucy's mother to obtain a place at the local secondary technical school, having pleaded that she was a vulnerable child from a one-parent family.

Lucy was also a keen and successful participant in the various school sports from netball to competitive running and she had represented the primary school in some of the town's competitive tournaments in athletics at the Sports Ground on the outskirts of the town, situated at the end of the electric tram route. What a pity then that neither of her parents ever found the time to come to the various events to support her.

The nearer she came to the school, the larger became the swelling surge of human beings as she joined a heaving mass of parents and prospective students heading eagerly to their new secondary College. Most were on the pavement totally blocking it for any would-be overtakers. As a consequence some families were aiming to overtake the commotion and were hazarding their safety by hastening towards the school on the side of the busy road.

A rising turmoil of conversation and intermittent sounds of hilarity and laughter grew as Lucy tried to slip her recently obtained smart-phone unobtrusively in her inside pocket. The nearer she came to the College, the more acutely she felt her solitary, vulnerable condition ever more bleakly. But she resisted the temptation to self-denial. She pulled herself upright, held her head high and tried to walk confidently and proudly.

Because she was afraid of losing her precious smart-phone, she had decided not to give it up but to secrete it in the inside pocket of her blazer. As she entered the gate of the school there were two teachers waiting to greet the students and a large notice reminding pupils about the smart-phone procedures and warning that it was forbidden to take smart phones, knives, vapes and drugs into the school, adding that there would be sanctions against any students trying to breach the regulations and take such objects into the school.

As she entered the school grounds she spied her friend from primary school, Shirley Buxton. She immediately felt happier about her new school and shed some of her misapprehension. Shirley had been accompanied to her first day at secondary school by her mother and father and Lucy waited inside the school gates until Shirley had kissed her mother and said goodbye to both parents for the day.

Brightly smiling Lucy immediately opened up the conversation.

"Hi Shirley! Good to see you! Do you know whose class you are in?"

"Yes, Mr Goodwood's. And you?"

Disappointed, Lucy responded flatly.

"Miss Moverley's"

With that exchange of information about each other's class location, the conversation then seemed to run out of steam. In any case they were straightway directed to different ends of the playground to join their school class group. There the teacher waited for the pupils, requested their names and ticked them off in the large hard-back register, which she held in her right hand. Miss Moverley greeted each student by name in a smiling, friendly and welcoming manner.

When all the expected students had registered their arrival, the boys and girls were politely requested to form separate lines and to follow the teacher. Dutifully they all formed up, girls first and then the boys into a long line of exactly thirty students. Silently they followed the teacher into the rear entrance of the school through a double door into the near end of what appeared to be a very long corridor with at least two sets of stairways leading presumably to an upstairs floor and further classrooms.

As soon as they had passed into the school they took a sharp left into a classroom whose walls were richly endowed with pictures and paintings, charts and diagrams, mathematical formulae and data. As well against the far wall on the sparse window-sills, some models of what appeared to be student work in wood and metalwork were exhibited. Most of the far side of the classroom comprised entirely of large openable double-glazed windows looking out onto the playing fields.

When they had all assembled at the front of the classroom, the teacher invited them to take one of the assembled pairs of independent desks, girls first and then the boys. There was a bit of a scramble but Lucy managed to obtain one of a pair of benches near the front of the room next to another girl. Only then was there once again the noise of excited but muted conversation to be heard as the couples introduced themselves to each other.

The rest of the morning was taken up with formalities, making their cardboard name boards and printing on them in large block capitals their full names. In smaller print was appended a list of the items such as textbooks and pens, which were housed in the desk and a further repetition of school rules and how to address the teachers and each other.

The morning, full of formalities about how to do this and that seemed to fly by very quickly and as an electric bell was rung for the end of morning school, the students were led en masse to the dining room where, with a teacher at the head of each table and the students from the other first-year classes they were served an excellent meal with a drink.

On completion of the meal they were allowed to go out into the lovely sunny but small playground even over-spilling onto the lush green playing fields, until the bell was sounded for the commencement of the afternoon session. Then the morning procedure for entry was repeated.

Several times during the lunch break Lucy tried to make contact in conversation with other students about a variety of topics. But she was rebuffed as all the others students seemed to be already engaged in groups from their former primary schools. She arrived, one of the very first students at her empty classroom rather early, and sat reading at her desk some of the texts that had been distributed before the lunch-break.

When Miss Moverley entered to find a solitary student studying her texts, she took it that this was an assiduous student and she treated Lucy as such forthwith. For example, she asked Lucy if she would like to be a book monitor and Lucy accepted with enthusiasm. This invitation was soon to prove a useful but not always advantageous means for Lucy to begin getting to know the other students and their main preoccupations. It also had a certain status.

Notwithstanding this step forward in her social contacts, at the end of the afternoon session, she left the classroom to see an orderly, clean and tidy corridor, lined by pictures on the walls, some photographs, some student-painted. At that time, the whole corridor was inhabited by well-behaved and largely silent first-year students in small clusters. They were all hastening in an orderly manner to reach the exit at the end of the school day and then to return home to share the experiences of the day with their parents.

To her at that time it seemed to be a heaven on earth and she yearned to return home to tell her Gran about it as soon as possible. Immediately outside the school, she wended her way wearily but speedily through the crowds of parents and students in a multitude of ear-splitting conversations on the playground.

On the pavements outside the College the noisy pandemonium continued briefly beyond the gates as she set out hurriedly for home, hoping that her Gran would, as usually happened, be waiting for her with a warm greeting and some well-earned refreshments.

Her Gran was in many ways a kind of surrogate mother to Lucy and she undertook most of the work for her granddaughter that would normally have been done by their mother. To Lucy her Gran was quite aged and had been diagnosed some years past with dementia. But neither her age nor her illness seemed to make any difference to her assiduous and devoted approach to looking after her dearest and sole grand-daughter. Only her memory seemed a little less retentive than previously.

It was thus during that first solitary walk home of the new academic year to what she expected might be a cold and empty house, if Gran had forgotten, that Lucy had her first brief chance meeting with a handsome young late-teenager called Yusuf Hussain. Though of course she did not know his name at that time.

The occasion was no more than a brief but warm exchange of 'hello' greetings. But for some reason his smiling and welcoming face and rhythmic voice became cemented in her mind. The incident did not immediately lodge in her mind as she weary-footed her way the final stretch back home.

Much to her great joy, when she arrived home and opened the front door, she was straightway greeted by the smiling face of her Gran with a big hug and a kiss. They always had plenty to say to each other and Gran asked her granddaughter straightway about her new College experiences.

"Welcome home, Lucy, Love! How did your first day at secondary school go? Did you make any new friends? How was your new teacher? Your orange juice and biscuits are ready on the table and I am starting to cook one of your favourite dishes for this evening's meal: cauliflower cheese, followed by treacle pudding and the special thick custard that you like!"

"Thanks, Gran. I have a lot of homework this evening so I had better get started and I may need some help."

"No problem! I'm here until your Mum gets back from work."

They chattered on for a further half an hour and finally Lucy, draining the final drops of apple juice, mentioned, with some sense of pride, the very brief episode with the handsome young man as she was returning from school that afternoon.

Gran's response was unusually peremptory but not explicit enough for Lucy and it set her 'thinking' as she went upstairs in a reflective mood to begin her first batch of homework from her new College.

"Just keep away from those handsome, smiling young men, Lass. Around here, they only want one thing."

Gran said as she turned her attention once again to preparing the evening meal.

By the time her mother finally returned home at about nine o'clock that evening, Lucy had already eaten her favourite meal, finished her homework, gone to bed and happily fallen fast asleep still seeking to extract the wisdom from her Gran's brief comment.

Chapter Two: Yusuf

Yusuf Hussain had just left College at the end of the preceding school year at the age of seventeen with a BTech level three subsidiary qualification and an A-Level in Arabic. He was recognised by teachers as an average performing student but a conscientious and hard worker as well. His forte was in sport, where he consistently gave excellent performances in his chosen sports of cricket in the Summer and football in the Winter.

Further, Yusuf was chairman of the College chess club for a protracted period. Socially too he was well-liked among fellow students and many of the members of the academic staff. He had eventually served a year as a College Prefect.

Two decades previously his family had come from the Punjab in Pakistan in response to requests from post-war English textile mills for additional workforce for the worker-depleted woollen textile industry. But the basic reason for the requests was because of the local shortage of workers willing to work the night turn, caring at the same time, for two machines in the local woollen textile mills of the large industrial cities and towns in the North of England.

The woollen textile industry as a whole was already in dire straits, however, when Yusuf's father joined the local woollen textile mill and along with many other such mills in the City the firm was now bankrupt and had effectively collapsed, mainly due to the rapid increase of cheap imports of finished cloth from Asian countries and the nascent recovery of the analogue industries in recovering Europe.

As a replacement job, his father had taken on new work as a conductor on the local trolley bus system, also suffering a shortage of workers at that time, partly due to the poor remuneration for the work. But shortly after his commencement of work in that occupation, the transport system with a separate conductor had, in turn, been replaced by a driver/conductor transport system, which did not require a separate conductor. Yusuf's father was made redundant and was unemployed once more.

The fact that Yusuf's father was now unemployed and drawing scant unemployment benefit led him and some of his fellow Pakistani workers into a life of indolence, bitterness at their host country and for some few crime.

Like many of his male Pakistani compatriots in Britain, with whom he lived in the same closely-knit slum neighbourhood, he was embittered and disillusioned. Moreover, with lots of spare time on his hands, including time for some rather illegal pleasures, like some of his neighbours he was drawn into very profitable sex crime. This work was enjoyable and also enabled him and others to hit back at the majority community, which he and they saw as discriminating against him and his kind both financially and socially.

During this period of family turmoil for Yusuf, his family, and especially his mother, who was very ambitious for him, had done all in their power to encourage him to stay on at school and to be successful there. When Yusuf regarded the lot of his father, he was attentive to the advice of his mother and he prospered.

Thus his achievements at primary school and later at the Secondary Technical College had been exemplary and he had prospered in both the academic and sporting sides of school life. He also made it as Captain of the successful College Chess Team, where he was seen by staff and students as a born leader.

Having finally left the college for the last time only a few short days ago, he was becoming bored already in the early days after the end of the College term for the long Summer break. He had not had an opportunity nor even the time to begin looking for a job of the kind that he was seeking to bridge him to a place at the local university for a B.Tech degree.

Instead he had been 'picked up' by his close friends from College and from the same ethnic background too. They had already made a decision when they met up with him and assured him that, as one of their mates, they would like to do him a favour. In fact they had a much more profitable and enjoyable job available for him than he could otherwise imagine or obtain, not least as an apprentice plumber during the vacation, and on his way to university.

Over a drink of Lassi with the young group of his former College friends all of Pakistani ethnic background in the front room of Ali's family, Yusuf, a rather sensitive and impressionable youngster, was subjected to intense and co-ordinated persuasion that what his mates were offering would certainly be more financially rewarding than the plumbing job he was originally envisaging as his vacation money earner previously. His proposed occupation they asserted counted for zilch in the outside British capitalist world and that's what he would receive for working in that job, whereas what they were offering him was a star job and an earner!

The other side of Yusuf's character was that he had an outgoing personality. He welcomed contact with other people of different backgrounds as an opportunity to quench his thirst for learning about how other people lived and the ideas that made them think out of their box. His mates played on this side of his persona too and assured him that he would be able to exercise that interest in the job they were suggesting as a favour to one of their mates.

His gullible nature, however, made him easy fodder for his former peer group at the Secondary Technical College and especially his clique of close buddies, Ali, Arfan, Kashir and Abdullah. Over the years he had become very close to them in the primary school as well as together at the Madrasah, where they spoke Urdu together.

In the criminal 'business' group that the young men had formed were as well a number of older men from the local Pakistani ethnic community, who had attached themselves in directing roles to the business established by the youngsters. That group of older men now included Yusuf's own unemployed and embittered father.

On leaving full-time education, the group of young men had combined to plan and establish a thriving grooming business involving young Caucasian girls in the City, where they lived, which was already even in its early stages showing a good healthy profit.

As the business expanded, two of the group's older members and two of the younger ones contributed as taxi drivers as well, in order to deliberately encounter, groom, coerce and threaten young girls into a life of endless sexual violence and unimaginable horror by a small group of members of the close-knit ethnic Pakistani community. Not by any means did the group represent a large number of members of that community.

As ill-luck for the victims would have it at the same time, this illegal activity was almost totally ignored by Police and Social Services. Due to a misplaced conceptual sense of fear and appeasement to and dread of having to defend themselves against accusations of racist prejudice, Islamophobia and ethnic scapegoating, and the damage that this would do to their reputation and the effectiveness of Policing in the area, they had deliberately turned an institutional blind eye.

These organisations disguised their actions by saying that the poor tortured sex victims involved were willing sex workers receiving payment for their services and earning well.

They were thus just plain common prostitutes. The Police camouflaged that smear with a malign attribution of willing sex workers to the victims, arresting some of them from time to time. Problem solved! They imagined!

The same false accusations were levelled by individuals and groups of men in cover organisations such as cliques and gangs from the same ethnic background and neighbourhood. Consequently all of the older men and some of the younger ones, but not Yusuf, seemed to have mistakenly well-grounded feelings of disdain and contempt for their young white female victims, who were all unjustly swept from the human race category and labelled 'whores'.

Some long years later, the explicit reasons for the inaction of the Police and Social Services in the 'sextortion' scandal were described and documented in subsequent official reports. In effect, at the time it was widely known that what both organisations alleged and feared, was that the local close-knit ethnic community, comprising predominantly of persons of Pakistani ethnic heritage, would consider that they were being scapegoated by these two official key organisations and would publicise their grievance in the media. To avoid the expected embarrassment their inaction seemed sufficient justification for the appeasement policy of the two public organisations.

The organisations of Police and Social Services were thus afraid of being labelled racist and Islamophobic by some of the other vociferous sometimes recreational 'recreational' organisations in the ethnic Pakistani minority communities in the town, thus reducing the effectiveness of the efforts to improve the lot of that community. All of this was conveyed to Yusuf as part of his thorough-going brainwashing in their next meeting at the home of Abdullah. Indeed he was now allowed to enter into the detailed planning of the Group's activities.

For example, although taxis played a very big role in the early days of the grooming business and the eventual sexual enslavement of the young white female victims, the criminal gang's favoured spot for the recruitment of girls and young women began to centre mainly on and around the large span of the Open-Air Market in the heart of the City and the adjoining public houses adjacent to the market in the town centre.

Yusuf was accompanied to the open-air market by his mates on numerous occasions, who flattered him by providing him with a pint of the local beverage and dish of mushy peas! That came with an instructional walk with one of the gang through the market illustrating how the grooming could commence: the pick-up points in fact.

Many local youngsters congregated in the Open-Air Market especially on Friday night and all day Saturday. Most of these youngsters, young girl victims, were exclusively from the poor white communities in the town's back-to-back slums.

It was there that some victims were recruited most weeks, often with the enticement of free drugs. In contrast, their main but not sole hub for the recruitment of customers to abuse their pool of young girls in their evil business was their own community.

In the presence of Yusuf, the group had recently decided that they needed to increase their profits and their personal incomes. This required an increase in the number of houses and number of victims had to be expanded as well and this was where Yusuf came into their sights. Ideal background for our purpose they concluded.

As part of this grand plan, the group decided to expand their catchment area of young female victims to the area around the primary school and the Secondary Technical Education College, both of which Yusuf had attended, recruiting especially in the period following the end of the school day. So close to his home and mostly only half a days' work the job seemed to appeal to Yusuf and he offered to try it out.

In his training for the new job he had been advised to look out especially for loners at the end of the day, that is girls walking home alone or in very small groups and roughly between the ages of eleven and sixteen. This was the major reason why they invited Yusuf to join them as he was leaving the College that

Summer for the final time and they were convinced that he thus knew the area well.

What's more, his Pakistani ethnic background also fitted one hundred percent as did the presence of his father advocating for him within the inner gang. It also seemed common sense to the gang that he should be offered the chance to join his former College pals in the business. They knew him well and they felt that they would be able to trust him. The dye was cast and the day that he met Lucy for the first time was his first supervised experience on duty.

Following him and observing from a distance was his supervisor from the core group, Arfan! After several efforts at each other's homes devoted to brainwashing their proposed new mate into their evil business, the other members of the criminal gang and eventually succeeding in easing him into their vile frame of mind about the young victims of the gang's highly lucrative business, the time had come to monitor him in practice.

With time and effort, they had at last convinced him that the victims, all young female members of the dominant white communities in the town's slum districts, who they alleged discriminated against them and their like, were worthless women and girls who merited no better a life than they were being offered by the generous criminal gang itself.

Now in their final meeting at Arfan's house, the other young members of the gang propped up their argument by assuring him that the gang's business was well-known and accepted in the official sources in the City. Why, even the Social Services Department and the Police Force in the City were of a similar mind to that of the gang about the worthless nature of these hopeless and insignificant 'tarts'.

They gave as an example the fact that some of the girls had recently been picked up by the Police, labelled as whores and prostitutes, given a warning and released. They quoted it as an example of the depth of the gang's influence. The plight of the illegally arrested girls was basically ignored because the perpetrators of their abuse were from a large, vociferous and influential minority in the City. This was just one further illustration, they argued to Yusuf of the power of the ethnic minority community in the town.

The young members of the criminal gang convinced Yusuf that the Police were of the view that the consequences of any pursuit by the Police of members of their criminal grooming gang were not worth the effort and would be counterproductive. Manifestly, the young gangsters contended, the Police Force feared running the danger of negative reactions from the community, which would be very prejudicial to the already very difficult task of policing the district.

It was clear, the gangsters argued to Yusuf, that the Police were clearly afraid that any action by them against the criminal group would be construed by the powerful minority community as a whole as Islamophobic and racist, making policing of that area of the City ever more difficult or maybe even impossible for some time in the future.

So, in any case, these women and girls were just not considered worth that risk by the Police. The youngsters reasoned this explanation as the basic reason for the ongoing lack of any action against themselves. And at the end of the day Yusuf was convinced.

As a consequence of this restraint the mantra that these women and girls of alleged ill-repute were in effect a waste of time, had now become a recurrent theme in the inbuilt defensive service attitudes and decisions of the Police and the judgment parameters of the criminal gangsters, who were grooming these young ladies, now including Yusuf.

No consideration was given by any party to the devastating and agonising consequences for the young ladies involved over a very long period of time.

Chapter Three: The College

What a difference! Lucy's first day of lessons in the College passed quickly and she was able to begin to explore some of the many dimensions of the school's populations, its student and teacher members and the favoured activities of each group. The question that most occupied her mind was, though, how she would be able to fit into what seemed to her at first to be a complex social and cultural context, some of which she was going to have to learn to avoid.

Increasingly and side by side with the work of the teachers, she observed in the ranks of the students what seemed to be a cancerous overabundance of different social media pursuits, some parts of which could be potentially physically and mentally corrupting or at least placing at risk the future lives of each and every student. After teaching, the surge of computer addiction on the part of the students had become the second major field of activity and information in the College, but the first outside. Sometimes the first inside as well!

There were many dimensions to the social fragmentation in both the teaching and student populations of the highly diverse and increasingly multicultural College. There were, for example, obvious divisions on the basis of social class background, religion and ethnicity, skin colour and subject specialisation and sports interests. But there were also other below the surface cults, which could be much more treacherous.

Encouraged by the unprecedented explosion on the internet of pornographic and misogynistic material, affording children with access to disturbing and unsuitable content. The College was also a kind of crucible for different sometimes competing peer group cults, including an exclusively male misogynistic one and a Trans group.

These 'cults' included several drug gangs related often to major drug cartels outside the College in one way or another, each of which was continually on the look-out for a means of access into the College, its staff and students. There were pornographic devotees, a social platform obsessed with dying and, one misogynistic cult with disproportionate harm to women students, one small cult of women students, dedicated to self-destruction and another male dominated cult, which contained strangulation imagery. Suicide was rare but not unknown in the College, as was stabbing, which sometimes took place in the College buildings themselves, sometimes on the playing fields outside the buildings.

These were all circulating in what was intended to be an exclusively educational environment from which smart phones were excluded! But even if correctly housed in a secure lockable compartment on entry, they were immediately available at the end of the College day and during the walk home. It was an obsession for all students from the youngest to the oldest for many hours each day.

One item of which the College was justifiably proud was the plaque on the wall at the entrance to the City's Secondary Technical Education College. It indicated that the institution had been personally inaugurated by the Right Honourable Helen Wilkinson, Minister of

Education at the time and before her premature and much lamented death.

The College was one of only a very small number of secondary technical education institutions, somewhat over one hundred and twenty overall countrywide, introduced as part of the efforts of the post-war Labour Government to honour the promise of the 1944 Education Act of secondary education for all, delivered through a tripartite system of modern, grammar and technical institutions. The College had been founded on a nineteenth century Technical College site in the City centre, but had been moved to a spacious open-field site in the early fifties.

The College's curriculum reflected the technical orientation of the education delivered with technical drawing, woodwork, metalwork, information technology and science at the core of the Year One curriculum for everyone.

The main but not exclusive foreign language taught was German, although it was possible to pick up Russian, French and Spanish later.

There was also a small special educational needs department in the College.

In a rapidly changing world, the College had received an approach a short time ago from a neighbouring Multi Academy Trust (MAT), comprising some thirty-six primary and secondary schools, the largest of which had a student body of sixteen hundred students. The Governing body thanked the Trust for the approach but wished to retain its full independence and relationships with local government for the time being at least.

The College student body with over two thousand students had been fairly culturally homogeneous on foundation in the centre of town, and comprised both male and female students, mainly from poorer and disadvantaged slum areas of the city. From the early forties, however, its ethnic dimensions began to change with increasing rapidity, as was the profile of the academic, kitchen, cleaning and other ancillary workers, support staff and the City surrounding the College.

With the move of the College to the outskirts to new premises with playing fields, a gymnasium, an art room, modern science laboratories etc. the College began to recruit more widely and became progressively more and more multicultural.

The move to the suburbs of the City and the new facilities also facilitated and reinforced the College's continuing commitment to the quality of its staff. All staff including the Principal were required to take part in professional refresher courses often organised in co-operation with and with the support of specialist staff from the local City University on a regular basis. There was a good and mutually beneficial relationship between the two educational institutions and some of the children of the University staff attended the College for their secondary education.

As part of the ongoing efforts to keep staff up-to-date, each year all members of staff were invited to a professional development interview with their online manager and a record was kept of their development programme, their accomplished programme and their next professional development objectives. This record was one factor taken into account in any promotion.

For her professional development interview, the Principal was interviewed by the Chair of the Board of Governors and one other member of a different sex from the Chair of the Governing Body. A very few staff were sometimes seconded for retraining at the local university for a complete rejig of their qualifications.

The newly appointed Principal of what had become the City's foremost Secondary Education College and Chair of the Academic Board was Mrs Sara Burnley Crowder. She was a member of a family, whose members had served the College over many years and generations of whose sons and daughters had been educated there. The new Principal herself had already served twenty years on the College staff latterly as head of the IT Department before becoming Chair of the Board.

Although the College was now situated on a spacious campus on the outskirts of the town, it was not immune to the tensions, dangers and influence of a rapidly changing city. Newly arrived legal migrants and those who had arrived in the country by less legal means raised new demands on the College, not least for additional assistance in learning the English language and the introduction of the newcomer students, of whatever original background, to traditional English values and academic discipline.

Just as there were concentrated neighbourhoods of settlement by particular ethnic groups in the City, these were reflected also in the College, and often became a source of friction and conflict inside and outside the College. Ethnic peer groups emerged in the College, which coerced anti-social behaviour on some of the other members of the student body and even antisocial behaviour as well. An increasing number of students were suffering psychological illnesses such as anxiety and acute fear, which spread for many adolescent students from different and, in some cases, antagonistic ethnic groups.

Sometimes students had been discovered weeping in the toilets due to ethnicity-based peer group antipathy, pressure and conflict. Side-by-side with drug-pushing, skin colour, based on sheer prejudice, was also emerging as a particular basis of conflict. Religious belief was also beginning to generate student conflict as was the right to fulfil religious duties appropriately and in one case with appropriate washing facilities. This was an increasingly vocal demand from several ethnic student groups and their families.

Associated with the ethnic pattern of a particular neighbourhood, organised criminal gangs had moved into the city as offsets from both international and regional groups, which were often in violent conflict over their patches and the target market for the trade of drugs and weapons. In the case of the international gangs this concentration of settlement reinforced the retention of some traditional values from the previous homeland, not least about the equality of boys and girls and men and women.

So, the repercussions of gang warfare in the City neighbourhoods were often reflected inside the College too with control and distribution of drugs and vapes to students a hot and conflictual topic. In fact, in spite of all the varied control measures introduced so far in the College, drugs were still being brought into the College presenting a particular problem for the Governing Body. Drugs imported through areas such as toilet windows often led to violence, injury and sometimes, but happily rarely, death on the 'trading floors' of the College.

A short time ago new regulations had once again required the redrafting and implementation of measures to control drugs and approval by the Governing Body of vapes, knives, guns and smart-phones, weapons, all of which we being illegally introduced into the College in increasing numbers. As a consequence, the re-regulation and implementation of the new regulations required a substantial additional allocation of staff and Governing Body hours with addition of a small amount of student prefect volunteer assistance.

Like all human systems the monitoring system, which included scanning devices for blades, vapes and guns, was not perfect and required regular evaluation and change and in a context where the scene was constantly changing, the customer base expanding and the providing criminal bodies were also rising in number and acumen.. For example, multigenerational drug taking in the home was constantly expanding with consequences for several sectors including not just education, but also medical health and social care services.

Contretemps between members of different gangs led sometimes to violence, hospitalisation and death. During the past academic year, two students had been stabbed to death in a dispute over drugs and a handful of others had been injured in gang warfare spilling in from the streets. But the impact on the other students was also incalculable and the form and gravity of the threats on the College, staff and student body were changing and intensifying all the time.

The next big threat of a major escalation spilling over into the College was the spread of handguns, imported as spare parts from the

USA, and easily and cheaply available on various web platforms.

An incident a few weeks ago, typical of the strategy of the gangs' ambition to penetrate the College was the transmission of drugs across the College boundaries during the morning break, at lunchtime and at the end of the day. The boundary comprised some fences, hedges and walls as well as broad metal and wooden gates.

An earlier effort by the Governors to monitor the boundary through the use of volunteer student prefects and staff with the support of Police Liaison Officers and to halt the delivery of drugs and vapes from a gang outside to student members of the same gang on the inside had proved to be not entirely effective and at the present time needed to be reconsidered and redesigned.

In the very recent past a further totally unforeseen threat had entered the College unheeded. As the number of Organised Crime Groups swelled and conflicts increased the big mafia gangs were recruiting students from the

College to be their pay-back executioners. If offence had been taken or a patch invaded or a deal had gone wrong, etc., etc., etc., revenge was felt to be needed to set the record straight.

Students were selected or proposed by fellow students in the same gang, offered the chance to be trained in handgun use, (in fact the training was minimal), offered a choice of drugs or cash in payment and directed whom they were required to neutralise. Sometimes the payment for a 'big' job could be in the hundreds of pounds.

The aim was to avoid evidence of any gang member's involvement with the crime when Police inquiries began. If caught in the act of attacking a gang member of an opposing group, the student executioner would normally be tortured and then summarily executed by the gang members, who had been the aim of the attack.

So in an external context of constant social and political change and increasing violence, the College was a miniature of that change, which impinged on the staff and its students in a multitude of different ways. This was the ambience in which both Lucy and Yusuf and been forced to study, although they had both survived due to the sterling support of Gran in Lucy's case and his devoted mother in Yusuf's case. They were among the College's many successes.

But the College was not entirely alone in its fight for its students. It had a number of advantages in its fight for tits students. It was fortunate in having the imaginative and untiring newly appointed Principal, Mrs Sara Burnley Crowder. She had placed at the front of her efforts the development of good relationships, with other major organisations within and without the City, which could be of assistance and support.

In conjunction with The Chief Constable, Sir Keith Bradley Jones, she had swiftly achieved the appointment of two Police Educational Liaison Officers and close relations the Police at many other levels. In connection the central administration of all schools in the City she had development close relations with the Local Authority Chief Education Officer, Dr Frank

Balbinski, who was very helpful in responding to calls for contributions to the College's staff development programme, IT and AI assistance. Equally she had good and active relations with the City Social services through the specialised officers and current Acting Head of the City's Social Services, Dr Sohan Modgil, This was found to be of particular assistance in dealing with the many different issues arising severally in Special Educational Needs. Relations with the Press and the Club life of many professional workers, such as the Lawyers, some with their own Practices were also not neglected.

In spite of the first-rate dedication and efforts for their charges of Principal Academic Staff and Governors to support and assist all students, however, many children were not coping and some were lost on the way. That left them at the end of their compulsory education with one a single option, namely to join the ranks of the existing million or so other NEETS in the country.

Chapter Four: The Pick-up Locations

The original locations, where the initial contact with young girl recruits to the criminal gang's sex business, colloquially called the spark point, had been established in the very centre of the City on the site of the large spread of the open-air market. The market included many stalls selling cheap goods, such as cheap clothing, tins of food, household goods, the odd butchers shop, home-made jams and some breads, tea-cakes and flat-cakes.

Similarly homespun sweets and chocolates 'like mum used to make', offered a very limited but a much sought-after range of allegedly inexpensive goods. There were also multiple small cafes, where youngsters liked to gather for a small dish of mushy peas, salt and vinegar. In fact these small cafes were a particularly important socialisation hub for youngsters precisely because they offered a very limited range of cheap snacks such as mushy peas and meat pie dishes, chips and soft drinks.

Enlivening the market further was additionally a relatively recently arrived small number of stalls offering special clothing, food and other goods from the many different and diverse ethnic minorities which had now settled in the City.

All the stalls and especially the cafes were afforded the benefit of voluminous waterproof parapluies so that customers were protected to some extent from the frequently inclement weather, regular showers of rain, or during the Winter, come rain, snow and sleet.

Most of the cafés were spread around the exterior of a stall serving-counter, where a large number of tall stools with footrests had been placed so that the seated customer could place his or her order and be served directly across the counter, pay for it and then consume it there.

The money received from the customer could then be taken to the safety of a cash machine inside the café, where the food was prepared and cooked as necessary. The arrangement thus made it much more difficult for any prospective theft to take place, although not impossible. Some few of the cafes had tables and chairs in close proximity to the counter as well and these were also protected from the main ravages of the unpredictable weather by waterproof umbrellas.

The jolly scene was complemented by lorries on the outskirts of the main market campus, drawn up with their rear doors wide open. The open doors provided a platform, from which cheap items of clothing, crockery and cutlery, other kitchen ware, tinned and home-made food, etc. were offered by barking salesmen offering the purchases of the century! These 'shops' were always very popular. But you needed to shop carefully!

Finally at weekends to help set the scene there was always at least one motorised grinder or barrel organ playing popular tunes and advertising events at fairs ('tides' they were called) in local parks. There was a real jolly holiday atmosphere at the market. But there was also a galaxy of threats.

The scene offered a very pleasant and friendly atmosphere, which proved attractive to all ages. Sadly it was also a particularly attractive haven for the young people of the town, who had a few pence to spend on a 'meal out'. In addition, for those with a little more cash in their pockets, there were two Public Houses, The Globe and

The Beehive, each with an outside area, where light drinks were served, or in intemperate weather, an alternative and smart interior arraignment of elegant plush chairs and tables, where alcoholic drinks could be purchased as well. It was also a rewarding situ for the local mobs.

In such a delightful scene and relaxed and pleasant atmosphere and to the sound of the happy voices of other youngsters, laughing, chatting and singing, there was a facilitating context for easy interchanges. Not least was that the ambience also provided as a basis for drug pushers and child groomers to exercise their wicked trades in ensnaring further child victims.

Tales of the market were vibrant in the College and it was this plethora of youth-oriented opportunities that also attracted Lucy and a couple of her new friends from the College, Louise and Patricia, for a Saturday visit. Sadly and more recently the Police Force had been hit with a string of allegations of cultural appeasement in a practice of discrimination against white job applicants. But not before she had received a thorough briefing about the place and its perils from Gran of course.

When they arrived nearby on the local trolley bus and walked into the area of the market decided to do a 'grand tour'. They looked round all the stores, listened to the 'spiel' of the van-salesmen and eventually decided to pause at one of the small cafes more or less in the centre of the market.

Attentive as always to her surroundings, Lucy began to notice the movements and actions of a small group of young men like bees to the flowers and from girl to girl. Lucy recalled her Gran's warning about 'such men', she called them predators, and as one approached their table smiling and offering free drinks, she brushed him off sharply and he swiftly departed and did not return.

After his departure her sharp gaze followed him from group of young girls to group of young girls until at last two of the girls clearly accepted an invitation, presumably for drinks and/or drugs in the Beehive with the man. She noticed successive small groups of young girls walking towards one or other or the two pubs.

Then she took particular note of one led by a handsome young man.

Was that the handsome young man, who bade her such a cordial good morning that day only a few days ago on the way home from her first day at the College? Were they some of the girls, whom she had noticed being shepherded by him to the Pub, that like her were in the first year groups. Although she could did not know it, she would never see some of them again at school? Bored by this time, she and her friends soon departed for sanity and safety again at the nearby trolley bus stop and home.

More recently the City's main gang of child groomers had begun recruiting male school leavers from the main Pakistani ethnic neighbourhood of the multicultural conurbation to train them how to pace the market unobtrusively in order to identify, groom and to recruit young girls at the Open Air Market for absorption into their evil market. The criminal gangs had a kind of identikit as to the type and age of the girls they were seeking to groom and instructions about how to keep well away from the local Police.

At the weekends a strong force of Police plodded the market regularly nonchalantly patrolling the open-air market, heedless to the crimes being planned and executed during their very passage there, not least when the market was packed with such a crowd of young people there as on Saturdays.

A little while back, it was one evening when the group was sharing out the loot from the last week's takings that Yusuf's father had cleverly manoeuvred an opening for his son, soon to leave school, to join the group.

The scheme that he convincingly proposed was for his son to begin to test out whether the area between and around the two educational institution, the primary schools and the College, might be a fruitful area for recruiting what he called 'the local whores'.

It sounded like a good idea and all existing members of the OCG agreed to give it a go on a provisional basis. That is how the naïve and inexperienced Yusuf found himself on that very first evening of his new endeavour on that very road between the two schools when he bade a warm 'hi!' to an attractive looking young girl, whom he did not know was called Lucy, almost as if he knew her. Had he perhaps observed her observant attention to himself or his mate as they as they carefully steered their first catch into the Pub on that warm Autumn Saturday in the Open Air Market that day?

Yusuf was now on a journey of no return down the slippery slope … ever downwards!

Chapter Five: Social Services

The normally unflappable Mrs Sarah Wozny, Executive Head of the Local Authority Social Services and Youth Work Departments was very incensed that morning. She was seriously concerned about what was happening to so many of the young people in her City and the massive and constantly changing avalanche of challenges the young people were having to live with every day of their lives.

She was dedicated to the idea that Social Services working co-operatively with others in the City such as the College, schools the MAT and the Police could attenuate many of the challenges and offer the City's students a better preparation for their future lives. True it would not be easy especially given the increasing number of OCGs, which were working in the City to generate the challenges that were in many cases life threatening and some even fatal.

This morning, however, more than anything else she was incensed by two letters, one with an attachment that she had found on her desk when she arrived that day. One was from an old woman and her granddaughter asking what response the Local Authority, Social Services and Children's Department were proposing to deal with the increasingly damaging issue of the grooming, abduction and sextortion of many young girls in the City by gangs of men from a particular ethnic group. The letter also contained a request for a meeting with her and her senior colleagues to discuss the matter further and consider analytically the evidence that she and her granddaughter had discovered so far.

The second letter was from the Mayor's office and the attachment had been sent with an urgent request that a response be prepared post haste for release to the media. On the basis of this 'somewhat more direct than usual' instruction from the Mayor, the Head of all Social Services in the City, Mrs Sarah Wozny, decided to call together a small working party of senior staff from her department to draw up an initial Press release for presentation to the Mayor and his colleagues. The letter from the grandmother and her granddaughter was swished into a tray labelled 'Pending'.

To draft an initial response to the Mayor's letter, she envisaged a working party of five senior members of staff, which would comprise two senior colleagues from Social Services and two from Youth Work with her as Chair. They would meet today, this morning if possible, and get a draft to the Mayor's Office before the end of the day.

She made a list of names for her Secretary and without further delay she called in her Secretary and asked her to circulate the letter from the Mayor and the attachment to all the senior staff that she had listed with an invitation to join her later that morning, say eleven o'clock, in her office to discuss the material and the Mayor's request.

Agitated, she closely scrutinised the Mayor's letter and the attachment once more. The attachment to the Mayor's letter was from what claimed to be an ethnic Pakistani charitable organisation that she had never encountered before. There was an unmistakeable whiff of hypocrisy about some of the claims the letter made but there was an element of truth in some of its statements.

She found herself having to do mental gymnastics to cope with how to respond. On the one hand there was a claim to a two-tier service towards the Pakistani ethnic population, with white areas of the City getting a better and more caring, responsive and close quarters deal than the Pakistani neighbourhood received.

She recognised the inevitable truth in this accommodation. Just in terms of the time spent with that ethnic group, their work had failed to anywhere near meet their needs. They had failed to meet frequently with the senior members of that neighbourhood, to listen and explain the kinds of services they could offer and what they could not offer. Almost totally they had not provided sufficient interpreter services in Urdu for the largely fairly newly arrived and increasingly voluminous community.

The Department had remained somewhat too distant from the Community and from the senior members and cultural leaders of the community to listen to their cares and to explain what the Department had to offer and to help them to understand what it could not offer and why.

On the other hand, the attachment censoriously but unfairly excoriated some of the recent actions of the Department. For example the letter criticised the role played by the Social Services Department in turning over to the City Police Force forty-two of the staff of seven brothels in the City, all of them from the Pakistani ethnic community displayed a massive gap in any understanding of English Law.

The rationale of the criticism was because of the claim made by all of the captives, apprehended during the raids that they were victims of modern slavery, who allegedly had been forced to work under conditions of slavery and had been apprehended when the brothels had been raided and closed down by the Police. Because of their very claim to modern slavery decision about their future, it required that all captives had been allocated to social services for a decision about their future. After time-consuming and costly detailed, medical and interview analysis and with the presence of interpreters, it had been decided by Social Services that they were all suspect of being complicit in crime and should therefore be allocated to the City's Police Force for further investigation and action if and when necessary.

Finally in the letter the intractable problem of whether state schools could legitimately provide washing facilities for Friday prayers for Muslim pupils and staff at school, was one to be passed straightway to the Chief Education Officer, Dr Frank Balbinski and the City's Department of Education.

There was scant information but the brothels appeared to have been established and were run by and under the influence of a small number of members of an organisation from the Pakistani ethnic community's neighbourhood in the Northwest of the City. It was not clear who the letter represented, if anyone apart from those, who had signed it.

She surmised that they did not in any way represent the rather conservative local Pakistani ethnic community.

The same document also contained a further shameful allegation that the local Police and Social Services in the City had shown a hostile attitude towards the City's own Muslim community in order to try to hide their own gross failures. This allegation was particularly advanced with regards to the treatment of child sex-groomers by her Department, something which was not just hurtful but untrue. She had to admit, however, that the performance of her colleagues had been far from sparkling in the Police mission to tackle the problem.

In his letter, the Mayor's office had added a caveat to the effect that it was not clear that the organisation responsible for the letter he had received had been sent with the support of the local ethnic Pakistani community as a whole, just by the elders or even a majority of the adult members. Thus the development should not necessarily be taken as representative of the view of that particular minority community.

When the senior staff joined together to prepare a response to the Mayor's letter and the attachment from the Ethnic Pakistani Youth Group and it had been read and digested by most of the senior staff of the Social Services Department, and indeed all staff in Social Services, the letter from the ethnic Pakistani Youth Organisation was universally condemned as outrageously biased and largely untrue.

But that was not enough for her sharp and evaluative mind. She felt that there might perhaps have been shortcomings in the way that her Department had related to the Ethnic Pakistani community at the time, which had broken down trust and communication between the community and the Police.

She felt that there was a sense of alienation in the letter and they had to respond positively on the basis of respect for all persons in all communities, which was her leitmotif. Her positive thinking was pre-empted, however, by the expressed views of other senior members of the assembled working party.

Led by Tom Grayson, Head of Physiotherapy at the Trust, astounding surprise was expressed by several staff that given the heinous sexual extortion which had occurred and the lives of so many hundreds of young girls destroyed, no organisation comprising members of any ethnic background whatsoever in the City should be seeking to justify that criminal and illegal conduct of the evil tormentors.

To seek to protect the perpetrators of such crimes from Justice as well was scandalous. He asked a fundamental question about what he described as the blatantly misogynous attitudes of the cowboys, who had written the letter.

"I find something distinctly misogynously medieval in the thinking behind this letter of complaint about the conduct of this Department. Did the writers of the letter not appreciate that the establishment and management or assistance in the management of a brothel was prohibited in England and that it is a criminal offence under the Sexual Offences Act of 1956? The crimes they are trying to defend their friends against are the Law of the land and has been so for half a century and more. That Law applies to everyone in the land."

Laura Shipley, Head of the Children and Families Section of the Department of Social Services intervened in support of what had just been said.

"I agree with what has just been expressed. The attachment to the Mayor's letter shows an outdated and quite honestly rather ignorant view of life in a modern multicultural society, where free speech in a hallowed value and men and women are equal. My heart breaks when I think of all these girls, who were sexually abused by the men from this ethnic group for so many years. They were all children with the whole of their lives before them. Sex with a minor is illegal in this country and it is a destroyer of lives, where it happens. But there is also something equally insidious lurking behind the letter, namely an attempt to support the introduction for one faith of a so-called 'blasphemy law' in Britain, such as exists in many authoritarian theocratic countries around the world, but which could infringe people's right to freedom of expression in a free society such as ours."

There were enthusiastic cries of "Here! Here!" from all other members of the small group and Mary Blackmore from Healthcare endorsed what had just been said.

"The very idea of a Blasphemy Law that could prevent fellow citizens from speaking out within the Law and against alleged crimes because they were committed by ethnic minority wrongdoers, who are Muslim, will be totally anathema to the vast majority of the population of this country. To seek to smear those who do not agree with them, with the aim of frightening and deterring those in authority from legitimate action by defaming them, is totally loathsome and unacceptable. Clearly such a Bill would never have a hope of being enacted by the British Parliament. The very concept of an Asian grooming gang, presumably including a Pakistani grooming gang, being attacked because it was Pakistani and Moslem was held to be an age-old trope about Muslims and Muslimness long ago. In Britain all citizens are equal before the Law.

All citizens are protected by the Law. All citizens are subject to the Law. I am proud that in this country we have freedom of religion and I am equally proud to have doctors and dentists, national and local civil servants and teachers and many other occupations filled by our friends and neighbours from a vast array of different ethnic backgrounds. Moreover the accusation that the Police were exploiting racism to try to counter a fear of the part of Police, Social Services and Education arms of the local Council was exactly what the writers were doing themselves."

She paused to emphasise what she wanted to say next.

"Subsequent official reports and investigations have clearly shown that what happened was exactly the opposite, namely that preferential tolerance was afforded to criminals from one particular minority ethnic group, who were criminally active and should have been jailed subject to just procedure by our Laws."

Sohan Modgil, Deputy Head of Social Services, contributed to the general expression of acclaim for the points of view being expressed.

"Yes, I agree! In fact, some three years ago a report by the City Council found that the fear of being thought racist and Islamophobic had inhibited the Police and Social Services in responding to sexual abuse allegations involving thousands of children abused by predominantly Pakistani Muslim men."

In agreement the debate continued with a concern for the City's children as Mrs Sarah Wozny, Executive Head of the Local Authority Social Services and Youth Work broadened the debate.

"It seems to me as if every new week is bringing a storm of accusations and ordeals for the youngsters of our City, whether in the guise of contaminated vapes, the spread of new more powerful and highly dangerous drugs, increasing multigenerational drug addiction in families, lack of adequate care for child addicts, inadequate hospitalisation and other accommodation for young drug addicts, increased conflict in relations between the youths of different ethnic communities in the City, evil, sometimes suicide-encouraging, transmissions on inadequately controlled internet social platforms, where some items are highly undesirable but not illegal. We are now faced with foolish assertions even praise that sexual grooming and forced sexual exploitation of young white females is, manifestly illegal, is praised and certainly even excused and even acclaimed by some particular ethnic minority males. And much else besides. These are and should be our major concerns in caring for our children"!

She proceeded to lengthen her list of potential challenges for children.

"All of these challenges for all of our children, whatever their ethnic or religious background, are amplified by escalating human problems of family break-up, gang-related knife and gun fights and deaths, low-level crime by young people such as shop-lifting, often facilitated by one or other of the criminal gangs in the City, sleeping rough and inadequate placement for young people needing to be social-housed not too far away from their family for various reasons and latterly the use of schoolchildren as executioners for the mafia criminals in our midst. The mind boggles!"

The Chief Finance Officer of the Department added a corollary to what the Head had said.

"To add to the necessary and sometimes urgent resource-demanding responses to the growing avalanche of problems amongst youngsters, our own Department is being hit with a static budget and staffing complement and totally inadequate opportunities to offer adequate staff in-service professional updating. Sick leave is increasing exponentially, some of it long-term without replacement. The changing cultural make-up of the wider population in the city is also in part bringing with it the need for the employment of translators and interpreters and demanding a changing face to the staff of the Department as well."

Tired of lamenting their problems, the group quickly came up with a beginning of their proposed Press Release, resting on the findings of the City's investigation into more or less the same phenomena and reactions some three years previously as they stated clearly.

"It is not unusual to find the charge of Islamophobia being used by Muslim wrongdoers or their allies in order to seek to smear and deter those who seek to bring wrongdoers to Justice, regardless of their religious or ethnic orientation. The decision by the Crown Prosecution Service to prosecute these men for their heinous crimes against young women were taken independently by that body and neither the City Council nor the Local Authority played any part in that process."

The proposed responsive letter added what all members of staff considered important.

Here and now and in the future we extend the hand of friendship and support to our ethnic Pakistani neighbours, our fellow citizens, and look forward to an early meeting with them with regard to how to help them improve their present lives and futures and those of themselves and their children in our fair city. In all these endeavours we are all committed to respect for all persons, no matter what religion, skin colour or other personal characteristics they manifestly come from. Equal treatment for all our neighbours is the major aspiration of all our work."

In the euphoria of their unity, the letter from an ordinary grandmother and her granddaughter, Lucy was forgotten at least for the moment.

Chapter Six: The Police

The Chief Constable, Sir Keith Bradley Jones was chairing the meeting of the large security committee, which as usual, had an overloaded agenda and a large membership. The aim of the meeting was obscured by an intricate web of different sub-issues all related in different ways to the health and welfare of young people in the City but requiring fundamentally different responses.

The focus of this particular meeting was promoted as a concentrated look at the wide and growing array of disadvantages faced by young people in the City, regarded from three different points of view. Firstly, in the light of the 2010 Equality Act, which aims to tackle illegal discrimination on the basis of age and other characteristics, the meeting would attempt to factually identify the responses that the City's Police Force was making to address the diverse and mounting challenges for children in the City's urban area, solely and in co-operation with other relevant organisations.

Secondly an attempt would be made to evaluate the effectiveness and suitability of those initiatives already in action and given the rapidity of change the evaluation of the likely responsiveness of those in planning in order to identify areas which needed updating or fundamental revision.

Thirdly an attempt would be made to identify any additional or revised approaches required to keep pace with the rapid and ever-changing spectrum of increasing demands and to seek co-operative responses to those challenges with other organisations at the City and neighbourhood levels. The unexpected passage in early 2025 of the legal definition of a woman by the Supreme Court was a good example of one of the factors that required sudden changes in all three domains.

For this reason a wide diversity of colleagues from CID, including Chief Superintendent Carol Lies-Brown, the head of the Police Education Liaison Service and the Chief Officer of the Police Forces' Drugs Squad were attending, as were the Chief Police AI Officer and an officer from the Family Liaison Service.

Also present were colleagues from outside organisations such as the Local Authority Social Services and Youth Work Departments and the NSPCC.

Against a background of tragically growing hospitalisation and death from drugs, contaminated vapes, knives guns, and self-harm by school children, the Local Authority Chief Education Officer, Dr Frank Balbinski, was also present with a bevy of specialised colleagues, including from the Multi-Academy Trust (MAT) with a geographically very widespread membership of some 35 Academies and a focus on educational Information Technology Services and more recently Artificial Intelligence (AI).

An executive paper had been prepared by the Chief Constable's team and it addressed the business of the meeting, suggested a structure for discussion and envisaged a series of combined outcomes. In the conceptual framework that it proposed was a series of conceptual headings, such as children and drugs, health and welfare services for children, sexual exploitation of children, educational support for children and young people up to the age of 18 years, relations between children and local business and industries and responses to children with a range of different special needs, including those in care from the City and placement by other designations and geographical areas of children by Local Authorities further afield.

In welcoming the participants to the meeting and emphasising the need for co-operative endeavour to successfully address the challenges facing young children in the City, the Chief Constable began his delivery with a courageous but critical comment about their joint work thus far.

"Our children face an unprecedented and extremely wide splay of problems and challenges in pursuing a normal life in this City at this time. There are some Wards where almost twenty percent of the population do not have a single educational qualification, and public services are being overwhelmed by newly arriving migrants. Subject to grooming and drug-inspired sexual exploitation many children, predominantly but not exclusively young girls, are abused for years and years in unending torment. Sometimes dousing with petrol has been used as a means used by their evil captors of obtaining compliance of the overseer or his client with the vile and perverse tastes of the client.

The IT systems of our internet, once so recently and powerfully helpful to children's education have in some cases been warped with an unprecedented explosion of pornographic and in some cases death-inducing and self-harm content. Social media are now in fact putting children's lives increasingly at risk with sometimes harmful, though not always illegal, cult suicide and self-harm material. The brunt but not the exclusivity of harm is falling on women and girls. There are massive skills shortages in the local economy at the same time as there is a severe shortage of businesses offering placements and mentoring to train up the many youngsters residing permanently in the NEETS system. Our joint and individual responses, including our communication with our neighbours in all neighbourhoods of the City, I think we will all agree, have been inadequate and tardy. Only one conclusion is clear. We are letting our children down. The big question today is thus what can we do better now, individually and perforce together, to help our children and fulfil their aspirations?"

Chief Superintendent Carol Lies-Brown, Head of the Police Force's CID, indicated a wish to support and refine what the Chief Constable had said.

"There is no doubt of the courageous accuracy of what the Chief Constable has shared with us this morning. With websites obsessed with dying and platforms still not obliged to remove illegal suicide and self-harm content, platforms selling everything from illegal drugs, to blades, tainted vapes and guns, with a harmful pro-suicide cult still permitted viewing, with the watering down of the present slowly proceeding 'Online Safety Bill', widespread misogyny and racial and ethnic prejudice, platforms still not currently obliged to remove illegal suicide and self-harm content, such as strangulation imagery, there is just so much disturbing and unsuitable content available to our young people, which should be firmly blocked and outlawed. If you add to all that, doom-scrolling on TikTok and Snapchat, there is little doubt that in the last five years social media have become ever more toxic and addictive, with an ever more devastating toll of consequential casualties. The Chief Constable' identification of the misfit between the needs of a growing population, its industries and businesses, on the one hand, and the availability of appropriate placement and training opportunities is also on the ball. We are failing to respond to the changing needs of our society including the need to retrofit and modernise large numbers of properties but with a numerical and qualitatively inadequate production of the qualified workers, bricklayers, plasters, electricians, plumbers, etc., needed for those middle level specialised jobs."

Dr Mohandas Patel, Deputy Head of the Local Authority's Social Services Department intervened to look at the impact of the same issues from a slightly different perspective.

"Colleagues! Sadly we live at a time and in a place of widespread cyber-stalking, grooming for sexual abuse of girls as young as eleven by gangs of exclusively or mostly Pakistani ethnic heritage background, facilitated gender-based violence, cyber harassment, cyber-bullying, on-line gender-based hate speech, intimate and non-consensual personal image abuse and transmission in generally addictive social media. These attacks have a wide range of impacts, on sleep for example, attention concentration, emotional stability and anxiety, work and study relationships with family and friends and the age of digital consent is hovering still at 13 years of age. It is my contention that all platforms should be immediately obliged to remove all illegal, suicide and self-harm content or suffer severe consequences such as they themselves are inflicting on thousands of vulnerable youngsters up and down the country and nearer home in our very own City."

The Chief Education Officer added one particular case of a growing menace to young girls in the city.

"Sir, if I may just add one particular evil criminal, gang-based attack on young white girls in our city, to which no one has referred so far. I refer to male gangs of ethnic Pakistani heritage, grooming ever increasing numbers of young girls from our schools in order to sexually abuse them for the rest of their young lives and often fatally impair any future successful existence. For overwhelmingly obvious reasons of community cohesion and the position of the vast majority of law-abiding British Muslims and the important contribution which they make to our national political, cultural and economic life, I would emphasise that although the Pakistani-heritage gangs appear to be all-Muslim, this does not mean that all Muslim groups are involved and culpable. Quite the reverse. The groups appear to be almost exclusively of men of Pakistani ethnic background. This is a criminal activity, which can and should be tackled and quickly eradicated in this city by the Police and its various community services. I would, therefore, ask this meeting to join with the Education Department in the efforts currently being made to bring these wicked men to justice and eradicate the evil damaging of so many young women's lives. Without fear or favour!"

Little by little it was becoming clear that the extent of willingness for co-operative working of the parties was sadly declining. This gap was due not solely to unwillingness by the various departments and organisations, many of whom saw this as an exclusively Police matter. It was added to as well by lack of funding and absence of sufficiently flexible staff time allocation to activities, which were seen as extraneous to the particular concern of each Force, Department, section or organisation.

The recently appointed Secondary Technical College Principal and Chair of the Academic Board, Mrs Celia Helen Chetwynd-Jones, was unwilling to leave that process of universal belly-aching, as she saw it, to remain the one achievement of the meeting and she spoke forcefully and convincingly of additional provision for children in cooperative working with other organisation, Public and Private.

"A short while ago, when I first had the good fortune to be appointed as Principal of the City's leading and largest Secondary Education College, it was amongst the lowest three educational achievers in the city. The College sat in a Ward with the highest proportion of young people not in employment, education or training, a stark difference in formal qualifications between our Ward and the best Wards in the City, and the widest gap of achievement in maths and science between male and female students. Resting on the basis of the legal duty of the College to assist youngsters aged 16 and 17 in the City to take part in education or training. On the advice of my Academic Board and with the enthusiastic support of staff and the full support of my colleagues on The College Board of Governors, I immediately established a series of working parties to deliver proposals to commence to address the specifically defined deficits from the start of the next academic year. One group, working with staff from our City University, established a plan to increase the numbers studying A Levels with particular emphasis on girls. The local bus company was also engaged to improve bus services for access to the College facilities for those who had left College. Working with the support of parents and the City Council's and Skills Service in accessing resources and making arrangements for things like accommodation, steps were taken by another group of staff to address the issue of the low aspirations of many students in a special micro-centre at the College, where students were counselled and arrangements made for them to attend short courses and/or do brief exploratory placements, while being mentored, monitored and supported by experienced staff."

She halted to draw breath and forged onwards with some details of the publicity strategy the College had adopted.

"Attractive recruitment publicity and inclusion of details in local newspapers, journals and local magazines and 'Voices' were complemented by agreed announcements, mailings and posterings of information at churches and recreational places where teenagers were known to be wont to gather. This all resulted in bumper recruitment to under-recruiting short courses and at the end of the year by decisions of over fifty percent of the students to register for formal A Level courses at the College, which in some cases were at the time under-recruiting. We are also rooting out any remaining traces of officer misogyny in the Force. There were many other successful initiatives as well, but I don't want to bore you or take up your time. I just wanted to say to you that together we do have the power and the skills to address cooperatively the problems we have talked about so much today. More information willingly from my office at the College. Volunteers welcome!"

There was general acclaim, even admiration for what the College was seen as doing and regarded as an exemplar for the some other educational organisations in the City. As the Principal sat down it was to the unusual sound of gentle and restrained applause in the meeting.

At this point the Chief Constable interposed an explanation of the apparently tardy and inadequate response to the City's grooming gang scandal, which had left in its trail the damaged lives of hundreds of young girls.

"By seeking to smear and attempting to deter the Police from investigating such odious criminal sex-crimes, a very small number of one community group have sought to frustrate the cause of justice in the shocking case of men of Pakistani background organising houses of prostitution comprising young white girls by grooming them, usually by drugs, into brothels. Some of these girls were as young as eleven years of age when they were abducted. The proposed initiative of the Police Force was maliciously interrupted by a false accusation. The leader of the City's Pakistani Youth Group, for example, is alleged to have asserted that the City's Police Force was unjustly typecasting the whole community of Pakistani ethnicity in the City and thus guilty of a racial smear attack on that Law-abiding community of Pakistani background as a whole. This malicious and contemptible lie had to be investigated by the IOPC, the Independent Office for Police Conduct, as the appropriate authority. Thus, a delay was caused in bringing these common gangsters and their followers to justice and more importantly arranging for the rescue and care of the young captive girls, who were in pressing need of counselling and medical assistance to attempt to avoid significant lifelong outcomes from their dreadful experiences. Multiple arrests have now been made and further action is underway against all those who profited from this dreadful undertaking either as providers or consumers. We will not be blackmailed into silence and inaction by a small racist pressure group making false accusations to protect criminals of whatever ethnicity."

The Chief Education Officer hastened to add a brief comment about the role of the City's education services in responding to the problem under discussion.

"Since this network of brothels for young girls was brought to light, extensive action has been taken by the Department and its various Departments, schools, colleagues and other institutions in the city. A thorough-going revision has been undertaken of the way that current curricula address the protection of young girls from this danger. Widespread initial and in-service retraining of teachers, administrative and supervisory staff has also be undertaken on a recurrent basis. Parents have also been circulated with appropriate information and invited to meetings alerting them to the dangers for their children and how to avoid them and to report any suspicious approaches directly to the Police."

The Chief of Police added that so far seven such brothels had been closed down and over 40 of the staff were currently in the Justice System facing a wide range of charges. But his wish to continue to place the actions of the Police Force in a positive light were disturbed by a somewhat agitated member of the Local Authority Social Services and Youth Work Departments by the name of Mrs Sarah Wozny.

"Chairman, if I may, I should like to refer to the high score of all Wards in the City with regards to the numbers of young people not in work, study or training. NEETS they are called. These are the youngsters, unhappy and jobless young men and women in need of appropriate training, work experience, and career advice to escape the benefits trap. Part of the work of the City Council's Employment and Skills Service includes provision of work experience and mentoring for such youngsters. However, there are insufficient places to provide an adequate supply of trained and skilled artisans to fulfil the demands from the market because of the shortage of places."

She paused for a moment to check her detailed notes and then continued.

"There is a serious and very damaging fissure in the market. One, but only one, of the reasons for this cleft is the absence of jobs at an appropriate level, due to rampant recruitment of so-called foreign skilled visa migrants, mostly from countries outside the EU. In the financial year 2023, for example, some 200,000 so-called skilled visas were issued on the basis of the allocation of skilled applicants from so-called competent sources. Some of the many so-called 'competent sources' were 56 Kebab Houses, which proliferately sponsored a large number of such people, 83 businesses with Halal in their name sponsored similarly and one butcher alone sponsored 918 such visas. So I guess there was not much work left for our young people to join at the regular legal wage rate for those jobs! A final comment! There are Wards in this great city and ancient City, where some twenty percent of the population have no qualification whatsoever!"

The Chief Constable, Sir Keith Bradley Jones graciously thanked Mrs Wozny for her spirited contribution and closed what to him had been a long and wearisome meeting and one which had been hijacked by other interests than his own. Consequently the meeting had concluded without definitive outcomes.

Chapter Seven: College Academic Board

The Principal of the City's foremost Secondary Education College and Chair of the Academic Board, Mrs Sara Burnley Crowder had called together a small subcommittee of members of the Academic Board to assess the policies introduced since her arrival to strengthen the College's measures for the support and protection of young people in the College.

Her family had a long tradition of service to the City's foremost college. Her mother and father had served similarly with one of them having been Chair of the Board of College Governors. She began informally, as the occasion seemed to demand.

"Welcome and thanks for attending. I thought it would be useful at the beginning of the new academic year to reflect on the major policies that the Board recommended to the Governors at the start of the last academic year and to reflect on what success they might have achieved towards our stated goal of making the College a better, safer and more learningful place for our wards and improving the aspirations and life chances of a wider spectrum of students, particularly those who are disadvantaged."

Dr Catherine Bartlett, senior science teacher of many years' experience and Deputy Principal, swiftly responded in support.

"Principal. I believe that the College's decision to exclude smart phones from the school for all students was about the best and incidentally the most popular decision ever both amongst staff and students that we could make. I wish I had a pound for every student, who said to me that they welcomed the regulation. They said they welcomed not being interrupted during lessons by messages on their apps and those of other students and spending all their breaks on their phones in a permanent state of digital anxiety. No one, not one student, said that they disliked or did not agree with the measure. Staff were similarly supportive even praising of the introduction of the restriction in their comments."

"I strongly agree with what the Deputy Principal has just said and I can confirm that was my experience too."

Johnny Middleton hazarded, as an ambitious and popular first-year teacher, who was very adept at speaking 'on the level' with students. He pressed on.

"But there still need to be some improvements at the edges so to speak, which need dealing with. And soon! There are also other problems as well that remain to be efficiently tackled as yet within the bounds of our competences."

Dr Mahmoud Khalil, a middle-aged physics teacher recruited some time ago from Pakistan sought to add more detailed comments.

"Yes, the theory, plan and implementation of our programmes this year were good. But the actual application was lacking in some crucial respects, meaning that it was not 100 percent effective and many students found that irksome and unfair."

"In what way?" The principal asked acceptingly but pressing the teacher gently.

The answer was swift.

"Well! All students and staff were circulated with a stern but courteous letter from yourself informing them that from the beginning of the Autumn term, smart phones would not be allowed into the College for any students at any age level. A letter to the same effect was sent to parents, emphasising that sensing devices would be placed at all entrances and that any infractions would be subject to severe sanctions. That was fine. But no sensing devices were placed in the toilets or changing rooms, through the windows of which devices were easily passed or exchanged especially by inventive young gang members. Much to the displeasure of the other students of course!"

The principal accepted the point straight away.

"Good point! So, we need to inform the caretaker that all such windows should forthwith be jarred open at a distance smaller than the smallest cell phone?"

"Yes and those strictures should explicitly apply to drugs, vapes, blades and unfortunately guns as well." Dr Khalil answered extending his critical comments. "And it should be clearer that the prohibitions applied to the whole terrain of the College, including recreational and sporting places."

The principal thanked Dr Khalil, accepted the points, noted them in her little black note-book and endorsed the health benefits to students from not being anchored to their mobiles all day and every day, including reduced platform anxiety.

She then wanted to move on to the next issue, as she saw it, namely the opportunities for those College leavers, who had left College, merely to enter the realms of the NEETS and were currently prey to drug pushers and habitation of the streets. Wasted lives! She went on to cite the huge economic loss to the country as well from such a maladroit system.

"Wasted and much needed economic assets for the country just thrown away!"

At that point Mary MacGregor, head of the 'fabric' section of the Domestic Science Department, intervened.

"Principal before we move on, there are two further issues that might be at the edges, to which Dr Khalil and others have referred. But for me they are central and are not being effectively addressed by us at the moment. The first problem, as I see it, is attendance, which has several dimensions. Firstly we have those, who now regularly think that because, consequent on working patterns of their parents during the epidemic, their parents are working a four-day week, they should only have to work four days themselves at College. Then there are those who just suddenly disappear and never return, predominantly girls. Imprecise rumours suggest that they have been snapped up for sex work by one or other of the evil mafia gangs in the City. We also have some, who take a short break and then return without any explanation. Finally, we are now in the middle of the Moslem month of Ramadan. Senior students are fasting during daylight and some feel the effects more seriously than others. In some cases the effect is that absence occurs. So they take random absences without any explanation being given because we have given them inadequate support at a time of stress. In addition to the issue of absence, there is a second issue, which is bugging me. If I may very briefly speak to this subject, there is the poisonous effects of the big social media companies feeding obnoxious and sometime toxic digital to young people. In my view these media companies must be forced to take responsibility for fuelling a damaging and sometimes fatal world for our youngsters. Sometimes this results in aberrant behaviour and a premature death. I am not sure how the College can deal with this myself. But I am convinced that act we must. Perhaps to begin with a letter from the Governors to the Minister about the problem might be a good starter. Thank you Principal and I'm very sorry for the rather long intervention."

The Principal reacted with her usual aplomb and courtesy.

"Thank you for that contribution, Mary. No problem! Points that need to be made. That is what this meeting is about. On the first, we do have defined procedures, for the implementation of which the form teacher is responsible. You are right and we need to have a protracted and serious look again at how they are working. On the second issue about the toxic behaviour of the big social media companies. I am unsure exactly what the College can do and I suggest that we ask for advice from the Board of Governors and perhaps with help of the University to search for good practice in other Colleges elsewhere."

There were several expression of "Here, Here" by members of staff.

Having completed her brief response to the points made by Mrs MacGregor and conscious that these two topics alone could take up the whole day and more, she continued with her attempt to acknowledge and implicitly to praise the role of those other organisations that had participated in making the programmes of the last year so successful.

"It has taken the co-operation and support of many colleagues from other organisations for us to achieve the success that we have. In co-operation with local businesses, the Local Authority Social Services and Youth Work Departments and the local University and with a small grant from The Department for Education in Westminster for publicity, some fifty students had opted to return to College for a continuation of their education for 'A' levels and hopefully afterwards for university. That was a great success!" She praised and carried straight on.

"As an alternative, a similar number of students, who had recently left the College, registered as part of our new programme for appropriate short courses and placements in order to train for middle-level technical professions, for example in the building trade, bricklaying, plastering, electrical work, etc., but also in commerce and retail. Once again the courses were free and based at the College and in workshops and an IT laboratory redesigned for that specific purpose but used by all students doing IT and Business at the College. The arrangement was found to be very multilaterally useful. Those registered for short courses and placements in industry and commerce at the College also benefited like all students from a free lunch with regular students in the College dining room."

She smiled at her colleagues and invited further contributions from other colleagues. Mr Southgate you wanted to add something?

John Southgate Head of the Humanities Department responded by asking if the College had sufficient spaces for the increased numbers of students, given the expected influx of students from the private sector consequent on the decision of Government to apply VAT to private school fees.

The principal's answer was surprising to some of her staff.

"Predictions of the State Sector being overwhelmed by a wave of parents moving their children to the State Sector of Education have been proved wrong and indeed more parents overall seem to have achieved their first choice of school in year seven in the State sector this year. The same applies throughout the City. In some places I understand that school have had to close because of inadequate numbers of students."

Mr Southgate asked a further question about the fulfilment of the aspirations of all NEETS.

"Congratulations, Principal, to all of those staff and students, especially the student Prefects, who have frequently volunteered for such things as boundary duties at breaks and at the end of the College day, as well as other non-paid tasks for their hard work and dedication. I am sure we are all very proud of them. No one could deny them their congratulations for their public spirit, which bodes well for the future. On the other hand, there is a huge volume of youth 'worklessness' out there. There are hundreds and hundreds of NEETS, living and sleeping on the pavements, without family or other backup, cheap prey for voracious drug peddlers and an early death. Most have no drive and no ambition and are wasting their young lives away, still out there waiting for some kind of help. Some will not survive today, others will be so comatose that they will recognise neither night nor day, right nor wrong, food nor hunger, what is good for them and what is not. I think that with respect we need to expand our programme, urgently widely and quickly in co-operation with our colleagues in other organisations. Indeed I feel there should be a City-wide effort."

The Principal was sympathetic to the emotion behind her colleague's statement and agreed with what he had said. But how was it going to be done? Where was the increased accommodation, staffing and resources going to come from? Apart from herself, already overburdened with responsibilities, existing and projected for the coming academic year, where were the new supervisory resources to be coming from? She asked herself quite genuinely. But she chose not to mention those future challenges but rather to endorse the sense of success and pride that she recognised and had pride in among the group.

"We have already made a good start and we shall be repeating for new students all the programmes offered this year. Across the coming vacation, together with colleagues from co-operating organisations, we shall be going out into the highways and byways, so to speak, to embrace more of the NEETS and to entice them to try what the College has to offer with a series of pre-term single day visits, again with a free lunch!"

She jested and smiled.

"We shall be scanning the ranks of staff and students soon in search of the additional volunteer hands to help us to achieve an even greater success in the coming year. Oh and by the way, I am informed that we shall be receiving a visit from Ofsted during the coming year as well!"

As the Principal was on the point of closing the meeting, Dr Catherine Bartlett, senior science teacher of many years' experience and much respected Assistant Deputy Principal, interrupted her to insert another aspect of the problems of young people in the City that had not been dealt with in the meeting nor in any actions of the previous academic year.

"Principal, if I may just briefly delay our departure today to refer to a problem, particularly focussed on young girls, which we have not yet had opportunity to address in detail. Particularly from the Jay Report on events in Rotherham some year ago now, but having occurred in other major and minor conurbations across the country as well, we know that there have occurred many heinous events, in which young girls were being groomed, coerced and threatened into a life of horrific and violent sexual exploitation and used most cruelly over many years. Almost universally at the time, reports of such evil events remained unheard by Police and Social Services. My question is do we have any evidence of such occurrences in our own fair city? Is there any action we should be taking to alert our staff and students and parents of the danger of any such a phenomenon here? What action should they take to alert the appropriate authorities if they have any firm information or evidence of such occurrences here?"

The principal responded appreciatively but circumspectly.

"Catherine, thank you very much for raising this issue. You are right. In Rotherham it took some thirty years for most of those responsible to be fully brought to justice and the menace recognised more generally. The lives of well over a thousand young women were ruined in one town alone. For myself, I have not had any evidence of the existence of such establishments here, but we do need to be alert. In pursuit of that objective, could you kindly propose this issue as a major subject on the agenda of the next Board of Governors' Meeting? Thank you very much for raising this matter. Very important!"

The Principal was about to close what had been a very long meeting when there was a further intervention, mainly because it was a newcomer member of staff, who wished to speak.

Dr Cecilia Swithenbank, a recent recruit to a senior position in the Science and Technology Department supported her colleagues in her usual forthright manner.

"Some good news to begin with! I am happy to confirm what the Principal had already said with regards to this College namely that it is also applicable to the rest of the country. The expected swamping of state school places at primary and secondary school levels, predicted to result from the imposition of VAT on Private Schools does not seem to have materialised as projected. Indeed many schools still have large numbers of vacancies for students post sixteen and some schools have had to close. On the other hand, I have to report that there are still serious skills shortages in this City and our efforts to assist are being frustrated. For example, we have tried to help by increasing the number of places we offer in the post-sixteen technical sector, which would also help in drawing on some of those young people, who would otherwise be destined to join the ranks of the other one million NEETS in the country. Sadly, our efforts are, however, currently impeded, because we have enormous difficulty in finding enough employers to provide placements and mentors as part of the training, which we offer. So the places are already available at little or no additional cost. The aspirations and ambitions of so many more of our youngsters could be fostered and the impact would be lifelong and also beneficial economically to the country. I have to say that we are at this time in detailed discussions with the City Chamber of Commerce to try to resolve this problem. I am hopeful. But now you know why thus far there are the training places at this College and elsewhere still empty and the skilled worker shortage in the City is still unaddressed. The shortage problem is, however, greater that just ours. As a consequence of our shortcoming, we are stealing often no more than allegedly skilled migrants from Africa and Asia importing them to solve our skills shortages? Do we ever consider the impact on the economy and finances of the developing country of our theft of their already school trained and paid for human resources?"

The Principal supported the two major issues raised by Dr Swithenbank and thanked her most warmly for raising them. She then closed the meeting on a note of satisfaction and pleasure at achievement by all members concerned, also expressing a modest concern for the next mountains to climb and those as yet undiscovered. With that ambivalence in her mind and in the minds of members the informal subcommittee meeting concluded.

Chapter Eight: The Second Encounter

By the beginning of the mid-term break at the College, Lucy was enjoying her new educational experience and the way that it was opening up a new worldview of learning and opportunities for her. She liked her class teacher, Miss Moverley, and Miss Moverley liked her and she was very helpful and supportive towards her. She was also beginning to make new girlfriends.

Indeed Lucy's world view had widened so far that she had begun to think very seriously of undertaking one of the College student visits to London or historic York or even as far away as Paris or Berlin and she had discussed the idea with her mentor, Gran, who was very enthusiastic but sad that she was 'too busy' to undertake any of them with Lucy.

The weight of homework she received each day was heavy and required multiple consultations with her eternally patient and knowledgeable Gran. But it was all worthwhile, even rewarding and she was sure that Gran was enjoying it as well, perhaps even re-living her own school experience all those years ago. The fact was that at the moment she was thoroughly enjoying her newfound College and surprisingly making new friends.

The new subjects she was learning like languages, domestic science, information technology and life sciences extended her life-view enormously and her new sports experiences included a wide spectrum covering cricket and football, chess, basket-ball and long distance running in the College team.

In addition, she had made a couple of new friends, Louise and Patricia, who were also in their first year at the College, though in different forms, with whom she could share her new experiences on the way home and sometimes serendipitously on the way to College in the morning.

Louise and Patricia were not the only friendly students that she had encountered, particularly in sessions of her sports activities, but she seemed to have a special affinity with them on the academic side. Indeed she enjoyed their company so much that she had decided to ask Gran that evening if the three of them could meet together at Lucy's home during the half term break to talk about their College homework projects.

Since the beginning of term the three girls had been returning home each evening along more or less the same route as each other. Today with their rucksacks heavy with their homework for the holiday, they were ambling untidily along the same route laughing and joking happily at the prospect of no College for a week or so.

Cheerfully they were making innocent fun of some of their teachers and the idiosyncratic aspects of the speech and behaviour of some of those teachers, occasionally breaking into raucous laughter and mockingly falling away from each other.

Suddenly, as if from behind a bush, but actually hastening along the pavement behind them to catch them up, who should appear but the handsome young Yusuf? Of course none of the three girls knew yet that was his name. Tagging along at the side of the girls, he accompanied them, waving and smiling at them and shouting at them merrily, which seemed to them to be rather eccentric behaviour.

"Well guess who we have here today! And it just so happens that I have a packet of new wraps of weed in my little satchel here today and they're free. But hush! Don't tell anyone!"

He pointed to a small satchel hanging from his shoulder to his right hand side and cheerily pulled out a few small packets from his satchel of what he said was weed.

"If you prefer vapes, I also have a small number of colours and flavours. You'll no doubt be having plenty of time for getting together during the holidays. Where better than in our very own excellent Youth Café just down the road here in Holborn Street. There lots of the neighbourhood's youngsters of your age, boys and girls, meet regularly and especially during the holidays and away from constant parental domination! Here's a flyer for free entry. Pop in some time. The first drink is free."

He handed a flyer to each of them and smiled benignly imagining that they would have problems of such dominance by their parents. After all everyone did, didn't they?

The reaction of the three girls was, however, a big shock!

"Go away and stop pestering us, silly boy!"

Lucy retorted to him dismissively on behalf of all three.

"We know what your game is and we also have our own places to meet during the holidays at each other's houses, thank you. It's free there as well!"

"OK. Have it your way, young lady. But the offer stays on the table."

He began to move away from them but turned and shouted.

"See you three young ladies around some time when you have come to your senses. If you go to the Neighbourhood Youth Café during the holidays, just mention my name for the first free round. Yusuf! I'm sure you'll enjoy the experience."

As he moved away from them to accost another group of youngsters further on, Louise, whose mother was French, aired in her native tongue a suggestion to visit the Café mentioned by the young man.

"Perhaps it might be a good idea to go together and have a look at this so-called Youth Café that the young man mentioned. No harm anyway. A free drink as well by the sounds of it. What do the two of you think?"

Lucy was not at all keen, although she had to admit to a certain gratification at having been approached. In any case she wanted to consult her Gran about the wisdom of such a visit. She voiced only a muted "Mm" in response and Patricia restrained her enthusiasm for the moment until she had had the chance to think further about it.

The subject was not mentioned again before they parted for their different destinations and agreed to keep in touch on their smart phones.

As usual, Gran was waiting expectantly for Lucy and her usual fare of a glass of apple juice and a couple of biscuits was waiting for her on the kitchen table. Immediately she entered the kitchen and after rather untidily discarding her baggage and outer clothing on a chair in the hall, she addressed her Gran with a question that was bugging her.

"Gran. Louise, Patricia and I met up with that handsome young man that I mentioned had approached me the other day. Actually he approached us out of the blue. He showed us some packets of what he said was weed, which he took out of a satchel he was carrying. He said it was a gift and free and then invited us to a Youth Café further down the road on Holborn Street. He said that lots of the young people from the neighbourhood often met there and especially during the holidays and the first drink is free. He said his name was Yusuf. What do you think?"

"I'd need to look into this further before giving a firm answer. But as a first response it sounds more than a little suspicious to me. But then I am always wary of anything that is offered allegedly free! Not least drugs. That stuff weed is in any case poison! Pure poison!" She iterated ferociously.

"I would put such a visit on hold until I have had a chance to ask around and to visit and assess the so-called Youth Café further."

"OK Gran! Agreed!" Lucy responded and Gran continued.

"On the other hand do go ahead and hold the proposed meetings with your girlfriends from the College here at home during the half-term holiday. I am sure your Mum will not object. Please go ahead from tomorrow, if you wish. I will be happy to provide something special for you all to eat and drink. If you wish we could open up about ten o'clock. After all it is holiday time and you are therefore entitled to stay in bed a little later."

She smiled sweetly with her final sentence.

Lucy decided to adopt Gran's proposals and informed her friends of the haven for them all at her home the following week. They could start on Monday at about ten o'clock, she advised them.

Not surprisingly, Gran's suggestion for a meeting place for the girls and free ready-made refreshments was quickly adopted as the norm during the whole of the remaining vacation. They met each day and helped each other with their homework amid lots of chortling stories about everything, anything and nothing.

In the meantime Gran began to plan how she would tackle her promised evaluation of the Youth Café and get back to them.

Chapter Nine: The Youth Café

During the weekend Lucy texted a note to her two friends to confirm the day and time of the commencement of their get-together at her home, at 10.00 am on Monday. She suggested that they could complete working on their College assignments in the morning with additional natterings of course, have lunch and go for a saunter round the town centre, especially the clothing shops, or as an alternative they could go to the mega shopping mall on the outskirts of town.

Alternatively and if people wanted there were also several museums in the city with special holiday exhibitions during the vacation: all within a short bus ride.

After further consultation with Gran she confirmed with her some similar kind of get-together for the whole of the following week, Monday to Friday. She also received a small allocation of spending money for travel and other out of pocket expenses from Gran together with an ancient and worn peggy purse and a little small change also from her Mum.

Shortly after ten o'clock on the Monday morning the group began to assemble and on arrival each of them was offered a drink and a choice of biscuits by Gran. When Louise and Patricia arrived they were accompanied by a further guest, also French, called Yvonne. After they had all assembled around the dining room table.

Lucy greeted them all, with a special word of welcome for Yvonne, and mapped out the pattern of activities she was suggesting for the week, namely school homework each morning, a light lunch, and then a visit in the afternoon to somewhere chosen and agreed by the group.

The Mega-Mall on the outskirts of town, and the shops in the town centre, together with two of the museums were quickly agreed and then Yvonne, with Louise's support suggested a visit to the Youth Café on the final day, Friday, or perhaps rather on Saturday, when it would be likely to be busier.

It could be a follow-up visit to the Youth Café suggested by that young man, Yusuf, in his brief encounter with the three girls the previous week, Louise argued, and they should be sure to use his name to claim their free drinks. The plan was quickly agreed and all the girls began their homework, although there were frequent, if brief, interruptions to the silence with one or other of the girls asking questions about issues in their homework tasks, not least the new field of Calculus or just wittily making a statement or putting a question.

On the whole, though, the atmosphere was very cooperative and everyone was willing to make a contribution seeking to help the other. It was particularly helpful to have the assistance of two of their number, both of whose mother tongue was French.

Gran sat in on some of the interchanges too when she was not occupied with her usual domestic duties and also took the opportunity to brush up some of her now ancient knowledge of the French language.

After the provision of a very light sandwich and fruit lunch accompanied by clear apple juice drink the girls departed for their first visit on this occasion to the Mega-Mall. It was a long bus-ride to the Mall on the outskirts of town and there were plenty of chances for chatter. Conversation continued without a break.

Yvonne the newcomer to the group, spoke very fluent English without an accent, and she lost no opportunity to mention their proposed visit to the Youth café, that she said she had visited once already. She was relentlessly praising it very highly, almost as though she had a share in it, Lucy thought rather suspiciously.

During the bus ride the spoke again and the Youth Café and eventually all willingly agreed to visiting the Youth Café on the following Saturday morning meeting at the entrance at ten am.

Meanwhile before she departed for the Mall, Lucy had shared with Gran the intention of the group to visit the Youth Café on the following Saturday and Gran realised that her exploration into the place had to commence very soon, straight away in fact, if it were to have any meaning.

Thus, after Lucy had returned home and her mother had returned from work, as it was on her route home, Gran impatiently decided to take a first look at the place, in spite of the late hour.

It was still light and there still remained a slight trace of the warmth of the late spring afternoon, when she left her daughter's house. As she was still a brisk walker with the help of a single walking stick, it took her no more than a quarter of an hour until she arrived at the well-lit entrance to the Youth Café.

There was little movement in or out at that time and she mounted the few steps at the entrance and entered the door to be faced by a rather muscular middle-aged gentleman, who immediately leapt up from the table he had been sitting at as if to defend his patch.

"I am sorry, Madam, but you cannot enter the Youth Café. As the name indicates, it is intended exclusively for young people. That's its title and its function. And that's that!"

He stated imperiously but politely.

"But I am young. It's just that I don't look it anymore." She pleaded humorously.

But the bouncer was having none of it. He advanced and exerted a gentle pressure on her chest with his right hand encouraging her to move back.

Gran reacted immediately, seeing this as her opportunity to change his mind.

"I must alert you, Sir, that you have just committed two breaches of the Law." She said with all the authority she could muster.

"Firstly, you have acted and spoken in an ageist manner thus breaching the Equality Act and secondly, you have assaulted me. I shall have to report these two incidents to the Police. What is your name?"

He withdrew his hand and paused. She added challengingly.

"The shame is that I only wanted to pop in quickly to the ladies toilet. Is it really worth all the trouble with the Law just to prevent my doing that?"

He seemed to relent a little perhaps envisaging a future for himself, where he would be identified as having caused an old lady to wet herself! It would not be good for the Youth Café either. He pondered to himself. It would be the end of his job! He imagined the consequences with mounting horror. Finally he decided to change his mind.

"Well I suppose, just this once, we could make an exception and allow you a free visit to the toilet. But no drinking, mind you. Straight in and out. You understand?"

"That's very generous of you!" She retorted patronisingly. "Thank you, Sir, very much indeed."

He stepped back, allowed her to pass him and indicated the lighted sign to the ladies toilet on the other side of the room, which is exactly what she wanted.

Taking a rather lengthy route and apparently avoiding disturbing people at any of the tables, she circumvented the furniture in the room before reaching the toilet door. She noted the condition of the ladies toilet, which was rather unkempt with some of toilet bowls rather dirty, two of the washbasins having the remains of human vomit on them and the waste baskets overflowing with discarded tissue and paper towels and strangely with the odd contraceptive spilled on to the floor.

She took several pictures with her smart phone, until a young woman entered the toilet and looked askance at Gran as she proceeded to the one remaining relatively clean wash-basin.

Gran knew that her time was up. She decided to leave the toilet before the young woman.

She smiled sweetly at the young lady and exited the toilet at a time when the bouncer at the door seemed to be preoccupied welcoming a noisy group of half-drunk youngsters. To her left she could see a sign for a private lounge and urged on by a sudden curiosity she quickly went to have a look.

What she saw there surprised her and made her resolve to counsel Lucy to avoid the place. There were young men and women in various postures and stages of undress with one or two in a state of passionate semi-naked activity. She took more photographs,

Suddenly, someone seized her elbow and jerked her round. The bouncer grasped her arm tightly and painfully and began to coerce her towards the exit.

"You lied! You old whore. Well, you will regret it! I can assure you."

He forced her towards the entrance and began to make as if aiming to push her down the steps, causing her to stumble as she resisted. In that split second her walking stick 'accidentally' made contact with the most delicate part of his body.

Consequently he had to let her go to the extent that his throw was not fully successful. Fortunately for Gran there was a short metal banister to the front door and she was able to grasp the rail to steady herself and descend slowly exiting the Youth Café safely and rapidly.

Before recommencing her walk home feeling that she had accomplished her task even if somewhat bruised by the bouncer's heavy hand, she made sure that she had not lost her phone in the rough and tumble. She found it safely lodged in her inside coat pocket.

The next day when the group came together about ten o'clock, Gran briefly took Lucy aside and quickly summarised her experiences of the previous evening for a moment, showing her the pictures on her smart phone and adding some canny advice about avoiding spiked drinks and handy young men, if she and her friends did eventually decide to go.

The rest of the week went more or less to plan and in their final encounter all the group expressed their warm appreciation to Gran for her constant provision of suitable refreshments.

By this time and encouraged particularly by Yvonne, the group had more or less come to an agreement to visit the Youth Café. Thus, leaving each other on Friday evening they agreed to meet the next day at eight o'clock in the evening at the entrance to the Youth Café.

Chapter Ten: A Visit to the Youth Café

As Lucy approached the steps at the entrance to the Youth Café, there was a crowd of young people surging around and an effervescence of quite loud conversation with some giggling, laughing and bubbly merriment. In such a turmoil it proved difficult to find one's friends. In the end, however, all the members of Lucy's group of friends were able to assemble and prepare to enter together.

Lucy encouraged them all to use the name Yusuf to smooth their entrance.

They presented a united front and proceeded to elbow their way to the entrance finally arriving at a barrier where two well-built bruisers were systematically body-searching all would-be entrants, male and female, and requesting each one to declare their age.

Eventually after the demeaning inspection, which the bruisers clearly relished and the mention of the name Yusuf did not eliminate, and a fatuous check on their declared ages, Lucy's group passed muster and dashed to find a table among the small number of still unoccupied tables at the periphery of the room.

They were immediately approached by a well-dressed waitress, who distributed a drinks menu to each of them as well as a separate food menu. She informed them that they could choose any drink they wished from the drinks menu and their first one was free. They didn't even need to mention the name Yusuf!

In spite of a warning from Lucy's Gran about the possibility of drink spiking, each of them chose a large alcoholic drink of wine, beer or cider regardless of the admonition for their very first order.

As the evening progressed the noise grew and the conduct in the café deteriorated ever more sharply. Male and female began to interact more closely. Bodily contact increased including inappropriate public touching and some items of clothing began to be discarded particularly by females. Groping became was commonplace and kissing extended to various destinations of the human body, but ever more exploratory, extravagant and long-lasting.

Lucy was getting a bit bored watching all of this disgraceful conduct, when suddenly as if out of the blue, Yusuf appeared carrying a chair and deposited himself next to her by pushing her chair to one side crowding it with the chair next to her, which was occupied by Yvonne.

"Evening all. Hope you are all enjoying yourselves. Glad you see you took advantage of my advice and my free drink, at last, Lucy my dear. Glad to see you here!"

Lucy thought he sounded quite tipsy if not downright drunk and she ignored him as far as she possibly could, consistent with the proximity of his chair to her legs. Being blocked in by Yvonne and her chair on the other side, she had little room to move.

It was at that moment that she felt him beginning to seek to grope her. At first she sensed the gentle touch of a hand running up her leg towards the top of her leg underneath her short skirt. It then sought to persevere somewhat higher.

She decided that urgent action was needed and looked for an instrument of defence. The fork she had would be using to eat to begin eating her food caught her eye as a potential defence weapon. She swiftly seized it and plunged it downwards firmly towards Yusuf's invasive hand.

Fortunately for Yusuf, the fork met two barriers: one was Lucy's skirt and the other was the table-cloth. So the instrument of defence did not pierce his hand. It merely bruised it as well as his self-confidence. In any case the reaction was the one desired by Lucy and he withdrew his hand nursing it indicating that he was in some pain.

To avert further such attempts at intrusive conduct, she excused herself simulating an urgent need to go to the ladies. She detoured, however, as her Gran had done before her, and looked into the private lounge, where all kinds of paired behaviour were taking place from groping, increasing nakedness down to penetration in various positions.

Thoroughly intrigued, she took a mountain of pictures on her smart phone. But perhaps she stayed too long because by the time she had decided to begin exiting the private lounge, one of the bruisers was leaving the group's table in her direction and Yvonne was sitting back down with the others, including Yusuf, at the table.

Lucy turned her face from the bruiser and slipped back into the ladies toilet. She let her hair down full to her shoulders and turned her jumper inside out. She noticed that one of the old sash windows in one of the far cubicles had been left unlocked and slightly ajar at the bottom.

Raising the window half way, she skilfully climbed though, pulled the window almost to the bottom again from the outside and quickly jumped the very short distance to the surface of the carpark behind the building.

She then walked unhurriedly round the Youth Café entering the same entrance as originally. There was no crowd and only one bruiser and he was engrossed in his I-player. He looked up as he saw her approaching. She smiled broadly at him calling to him that she sixteen. Well she nearly was by this time. Thirteen at least.

Finally she joined the group again at the table, much to Yvonne's surprise. By this time the group had had enough of the loud music and bizarre behaviour, which they were surrounded by even in their own part of the café and they unanimously decided to go home for another free drink there.

Had the brief experience been worthwhile? Unanimously no!

Would they go back some other evening?

Maybe! And maybe not!

Without knowing it, they had avoided the first step, which would have led them quickly to drugs and sexual slavery sine die. They had also collected evidence that could perhaps persuade the Police or Social Services to see what was going on and perhaps to take the matter further. Or so they thought!

The next time she met Gran, she related her story and shared her photographs with her and they agreed that they had a responsibility to alert the Police and Social Services to what was going on the so-called Youth café. They surmised that it should be easy to find a website for an approach for both organisation on the computer, a task that they could commence their task the following day, a Sunday. How wrong thy were in their surmise!

Chapter Eleven: Frustrations and a Shock

The next time they met at home with the others, over a cup of tea and a couple of ginger nuts, Gran and Lucy conferred with the other members of the young group of friends about their experiences and impressions of what they had seen at the Youth Café.

As usual Gran seized the first word and came in very strongly for the view that what they had seen was illegal conduct and that was definitely underlined by the fact that some of the conduct it was performed with the acquiescence or coercion of clearly under-age maybe even drunken or drugged youngsters, with minors in fact.

She strongly advised that what they had seen and experienced should be reported to the Law. It was an obligation and particularly as many of the females involved appeared to be substantially under-age and it might reasonably be assumed that some of their participation was under one kind of coercion or another.

Lucy forcefully supported her Gran, endorsing Gran's view that much of the activity in the Youth Café was illegal and should be reported to the Police. But there were others who were unsure of the wisdom of such a move and they were surprisingly stalwartly led by Yvonne. Her comments about the lack of wisdom in such action and the dangers associated with it were convincing to say the least.

At the end of the get-together, there was still no unified view in the group, but given the weight of Yvonne's arguments against making a report to the Police and the lukewarm attitude of the others, the idea was rejected. An attempt at unison suggesting a report to the Local Authorities Social Services Department, not the Police, also found no group-wide favour.

By the end of the meeting after dispersal, Gran and Lucy, who had seen and taken many photographs of the 'goings-on' in the private lounge were of a fundamentally different opinion. They decided to try to take the matter further without the involvement of the others and they involved the others of their decision.

They still considered that the actions they had seen and recorded were at least in part and in some cases against the Law. There was, therefore, a clear legal obligation to make a report to the Police. The large number of photographs also convinced them that the pictures would provide powerful evidence for their contentions. But they were not going to alert their decision, when they would begin, to the others.

Even so, whether by a slip of the tongue, a body gesture or facial expression it was perhaps inevitable that their decision to consult with the Police seeped out beyond the group's members and eventually ended up in the hands of the very group that was organising the Youth Café and its fiery boss, who were responsible for the lucrative establishment and the attached money-spinning trade in grooming, trafficking and child sexual exploitation.

With that the die was cast for some kind of retaliation against the two dissenters as soon as possible! Sadly the two of them ignored or were unaware of the leakage and its potential for danger to them and they just ploughed ahead irrespective.

But the Head of the Cartel was not at all so slow-moving or inert. He saw this as an immediate threat to him and his business. He reacted immediately he heard of the proposal, and he called together his inner team. When they had assembled he explained the threat to his mates. He followed up promptly by giving the order to two of his musclemen for the priority elimination of the threat. It was he said a well-paid job of great urgency, but with discretion of course.

For her part, Gran got to work immediately on how to make such a report to the Police and Social Service, such as she and Lucy envisaged. When she began looking up the answers to their basic questions on her computer, she found the information about how to report child sexual exploitation opaque, confusing, profusely complex and unhelpful.

On consulting the words child sexual exploitation on her computer, she was confronted with a whole series of claims about who was the one to consult and which of each organisation's sub-departments should be approached first. Especially problematic was an apparent competition amongst The Police, Social Services and the old-established National Society for the Prevention of Cruelty to Children (NSPCC). It was totally unclear! Totally unhelpful!

Finally she surrendered and contacted the main Police Station in the City Centre, which referred her back to the local neighbourhood Police Unit. At the Neighbourhood Sub-Station, Sergeant Mahmood Khalil, the supervising officer for the neighbourhood, where the Youth Cafe was situated, was not sure that the things that Gran and Lucy were describing to him were the kinds of issues that he should be dealing with. He was a conscientious and modest Officer but he was conscious that the oral report and at glance the photographs were very sensitive.

It clearly demanded an expertise that he judged himself not to possess. In sum, he did not have any qualification, training or experience in child sexual exploitation. But he had to admit that it frightened him a bit and he agreed that it was a very serious matter.

So, notwithstanding his personal reservations, the Policeman felt that it was his duty to process the matter and facilitate its consideration by the Force. Given the age of Gran and the youth of

Lucy he courteously agreed to meet them at their home.

In his usual meticulous manner, he envisaged in advance that if necessary, after hearing their evidence in detail and examining the photographs with greater specificity and having a chance to question two of them about their experiences and pictures, he would consider very seriously referring the material upwards. That would mean direct contact with to the District Supervising Officer, his immediate superior, District Supervising Officer, Inspector David McGee.

When he arrived Gran opened the door, greeted him warmly and offered him a cup of tea or coffee and a biscuit. He declined the offer, explaining that he was on duty and it was also the time of the Holy Month of Ramadan and he was fasting from dawn to dusk, during the hours of daylight in fact. He politely removed his service cap and placed it under his arm.

As he entered into the front room of the house, he showed his Photo-ID to each one of them in turn. Gran gestured to a seat in one of the two comfy armchairs for him to sit down. After sitting down he took out his note-book, showed them a recording mobile and asked if they be happy for him to record their conversation. They agreed to his request and he proceeded to listen very attentively to their descriptions of what they had seen, intervening only once or twice about the exact locations described

Gran then handed him both sets of photographs, which he examined meticulously, numbered and then duplicated. He also gave particular attention to their sets of photographs, which had been taken in the Private lounge in some detail, in spite of finding them somewhat distasteful, even repulsive.

Before returning them to Gran, he complemented in an admiring manner to her and Lucy about the quality of the photographs they had taken. He stated that his own view was that the photographs definitely offered potential evidence of the value the contents could play in any prosecutions that might eventuate later.

He then addressed the two of them further.

"One thing is very clear from these photographs and endorsed by your oral descriptions, namely that they describe a series of serious and in some cases horrific cases of the exploitation of under-age females being molested and abused by older men for the gratification of these latter men. So firstly, as a father of three girls, thank you for bringing these illegal actions of grossly inhumane and sexual cruelty to the attention of your local Constabulary. Having confirmed my feelings, I have to inform you that the case is obviously way above my pay-grade and I shall need to push this upwards to my District Supervising Officer, Inspector David McGee. I shall also let him have a copy of my notes on our meeting today. With your permission, I should also like to let him have a copy of your particulars, including full name and address, landline number, e-mail address, if you could kindly let me have them before I leave. He should be in touch shortly to let you know what is happening, and where we go from here. I can assure you that you will definitely be called upon again and questioned about your recollection of the events and the accuracy of your statements and photo-accounts as to what was actually taking place. A bit of a nuisance if you are called to Police Headquarters but this case has now moved up the ladder and beyond just a neighbourhood matter and probably other specialised units of the Police will need to become involved. A bit of a nuisance perhaps. But you do have a bus-pass, don't you?"

Gran nodded her assent and he then asked.

"Is that all acceptable to both of you, then?"

On behalf of both of them, Gran responded positively to his last question and appreciatively to the rest. She assured him further.

"We will assist in whatever way we can in the pursuit of this matter. We hope to hear from Inspector Magee very shortly, as dozens of under-age young women are currently suffering unimaginably horrific exploitation for every moment of our delay. Thank you Sergeant Khalil for coming to meet us at home. Very helpful at my advanced age."

"No problem and you both have a nice day!"

He said cordially rising from his chair and making ready to depart

"The same to you." Gran and Lucy answered together happily, feeling that the meeting had meant some real progress.

So with that mutual salutation the meeting ended and the Sergeant departed.

Given the urgency of the crimes at the Youth Café that they had both portrayed in words and demonstrated in pictures, Gran and Lucy expected an early response. They waited anxiously. They waited, and they waited as the days and weeks passed by without any further communication from the Police.

Finally they decided to contact Sergeant Khalil and so they rang the special contact number at the Neighbourhood Police Station, which he had given them. But when they rang, they found that number had been terminated and all calls were being rerouted to the receptionist. They were, however, thirteenth in the queue!

When the receptionist did finally reply, they were informed that Sergeant Khalil had been transferred and no longer worked at the Neighbourhood Station. Further she informed them that a replacement, although appointed, had not yet arrived.

Asked about the information they had shared with him, they were told that the receptionist could not share confidential details over the telephone. So they requested a number for Inspector McGee, the District Inspector, and finally they achieved a breakthrough.

It was the Inspector's assistant that responded to their call to Inspector McGee. She informed them the Inspector was out of the office on a case at the moment, but that if they rang again towards the end of the day, they would probably be able to speak with him. Would Gran like to leave her name, address and telephone number and details of what it was that she wished to speak to him about?

Fearing a leakage of confidential information, Gran declined to leave details of the proposed subject of the intended call but merely indicated that Sergeant Khalil had sent a summary of their submissions to the Inspector about a series of cases of child sexual exploitation in the area, perhaps even applicable across the City.

Maybe it was that final phrase that compelled a swift response, because with profuse apologies a rather tired-sounding Inspector McGee rang unexpectedly at five thirty that very same afternoon and apologised profusely for the delay on a matter, which he agreed was very important.

"Look I am so sorry that I have not been in touch. It has been like a madhouse here. We are so short of staff due to the cutbacks and I have not had chance to read your portfolio in detail and thus to decide which direction to send it in. I promise that I shall read it again fully tomorrow and ring you again about the same time tomorrow, if that is convenient to you two?"

"Yes, that's fine for both of us." Gran replied curtly, somewhat upset about the inordinate delays, which the Inspector had caused.

Miracles do sometimes happen and exactly as promised, the Inspector rang back the following evening at about the same time as he had promised.

"Thank you and Lucy for all the valuable work you have put into this very important matter. I should like to meet the two of you with some urgency. If necessary I am quite happy to come to your home address. I could be there at about five thirty tomorrow evening again if that suits your convenience. I have the address here from the Sergeant and if I could just check it with you?"

He read the address and having confirmed it he rang off politely but rather hurriedly.

At exactly five thirty the following afternoon the doorbell rang.

When Gran opened the door, she saw a rather handsome young man in Police uniform on her door-step. Taking out his photo-ID and holding it up for verification, he straightway introduced himself as Inspector Magee. He was immediately invited in by a broadly smiling Gran, backed up by the now adolescent but equally smiling Lucy. In the hall, he was offered the usual fare, a cup of tea or coffee with a biscuit. But he politely declined the offer.

They all retired to the front lounge and the Inspector was invited to take a seat in one of the comfortable armchairs. He took off his cap, sat down and retrieved his notebook and biro from his pocket. He began by asking what he obviously regarded as a fundamental question. It was one that neither Gran nor Lucy had considered before.

"Well, I have read and re-read with mounting horror and disgust Sergeant Khalil's summary account of his meeting with you and the evidential material that you shared with him. I must say that I am really very impressed with what you have done. Thank you both very much indeed. Well done, if I may say so and thank you very much for all your hard work. If I may, could I just ask you whether you requested any permission from the management of the Youth Café to take the photographs that you took in the Café?"

Gran and Lucy were flabbergasted by the question and for a moment Gran was struck into a furious silence. Then she recovered and answered resolutely.

"No! We did not. For to do so would have resulted inevitably in our violent ejection from the premises. After all they must have known that they were supporting illegal activities for many minors on their premises. Gran continued resolutely.

"No! It was clear at the Neighbourhood Police Station that, what we could see with our bare eyes that they were facilitating illegal acts by coercing underage females into sexual exploitation for financial gain. If that is not illegal, I don't know what is."

The Inspector retorted straightway coolly and calmly.

"The problem with your oral and visual evidence is that it was collection without any say-so and it involved both adult and child components, collected by an adult and a child. That background could reduce or expunge its evidential value for prosecution. Secondly we shall have to discuss with the Local Authority Social Services Department, who should take on the task of pursing this matter, or whether we should share it and if so how."

Gran was horrified at what she saw as further blatant procrastination and she exploded Like Lucy had never seen her do before.

"Sir, with all due respect! These children are at this very moment continuing to suffer indescribably horrific abuse and their lives are being abused for money and in some cases maybe their lives will be totally destroyed. Their suffering to be ended immediately."

The inspector's reply was again cool, calm and collected.

"Madam. I do understand your justified impatience over this matter, to which I admit I have sadly contributed. I apologise once more and I shall try to make up for that lapse on my part by expediting as quickly as humanly possible the transition to the action phase. But unless we conduct our investigation with attention to what is legal, our attempt to bring these wicked men to justice and the whole case even could go astray and fail. The showing of your impatience will I hope help the case. So I hope that I can assuage your impatience a little this evening. Immediately I arrive back at the Central Police Station today I shall draft out a submission of the issues you are raising for my immediate superior in the Force and transmit it to her for urgent and priority attention. I'll let you know immediately I receive a response. As you probably now realise there are wider issues to be considered here about how to make sure that any prosecution using your oral testimony and visual shots leads to a successful prosecution of these wicked men. You probably realise now that there are wider implications of the case that you maybe had not thought of before. Anyway you do not mention them at any point in your reports. For example, there is a very sensitive community dimension, which will need to be dealt with at a level of great delicacy. Under-age exclusively white girls being groomed, coerced and threatened into a life of sexual violence by gangs of males of Pakistani ethnic heritage is, I am sure you have become aware, an extremely volatile issue and rumours are already spreading that the local Pakistani Youth Group is preparing fiery publications including allegations of Islamophobia and racism in defence of their fellow criminal citizens for release to the Press. Rest assured! I shall definitely let you know just as soon as I receive a reply from my colleagues at Headquarters and hopefully with information about your further participation in the case."

With that pontification, he rose somewhat petulantly replaced his cap and placed his notebook and biro in his pocket and then made as if to exit the room. He turned, bade Gran and Lucy good night and affectedly made for the front door. Gran followed in the Inspector's wake but could not keep up with him. She arrived at the open front door just in time to call a warm thank you to him as he was getting into the Police car.

"Good night Inspector and thank you for coming. We look forward to hearing from you."

Lucy had remained in the house in the hallway, contemplating how much time this had all taken away from the completion of her important remaining homework across the weekend. She was a model student now in the advanced Alpha class preparing for an advance in the date of her examinations and she had never been late with the submission of her homework before.

Suddenly she heard two dull thuds in front of her followed by silence. She looked up and observed Gran slowly slipping down to rest on the front steps of the house. She rushed to the open front door thinking that Gran may have tripped or fallen accidentally, only to find her lifeless and still, spread-eagled on the front steps with what on closer examination proved to be two small holes in her forehead. She was clearly dead!

The Inspector had already launched himself from his car to see if any assistance could be given and was storming up the drive at the same time using his official mobile to urgently summon an ambulance and the Major Incidents Unit. But sadly in vain! Life for Lucy had suddenly changed irrevocably and it would never be the same again.

Chapter Twelve: The Newspaper Reporter

The shattering trauma suffered by Lucy was not something that was going to depart swiftly. Gran would, and could, never be replaced. It would require perhaps many months of expert psychological assistance and rehabilitation to help to put her firmly back on her chosen career track. But there were some compensations.

Lucy's mother, a trained psychologist, arrived at the house mid-morning the next day with several suitcases and boxes and indicated to Lucy that she had separated from her boyfriend and would be living with Lucy now … and forever. She would always be there for her! No matter what! Like mother like daughter!

She explained that she would liaise with the headmistress and class teacher at Lucy's school to make sure that she had all the academic support and information that she needed to keep up the momentum of her preparations for the examinations, which she hoped would help her secure a place in a Medical School less than three years hence now.

Her mother would also make sure that Lucy's recovery programme was well-designed and adequate to her needs.

Her mother added lovingly holding Lucy tight.

Any household matters, like washing and ironing, cleaning the house, shopping for food, cooking and washing up will be taken care of in execution and payment by me on a one hundred percent basis and as soon as Lucy wished. A cleaner will also be taken on to assist me with some of that work and, with regard to the garden, I shall seek to employ a gardener and for the exterior windows a window cleaner will be employed and paid for my me."

Furthermore, her mother explained, Lucy would be able to invite her friends from school for chit-chats and her mother would facilitate those meetings and provide appropriate refreshments for everyone, who came.

Lucy could do no more than express a very sincere but short word of thanks and appreciation.

Things seemed to be going smoothly for some two weeks after Gran's funeral and Lucy seemed to be picking up more rapidly now. One day there was a knock at the front door heralding another positive surprise. Her mother went to answer and on opening the door she discovered in front of her a young and very attractive and well-dressed woman with a Press badge attached to her lapel of the local 'Herald' Newspaper.

The lady politely asked if she could have a quick word with Lucy, saying that she was reading and digesting the testaments that Lucy and Gran had compiled about the sex exploitation scandal in the City.

Fearing that it might be too much for Lucy so soon after Gran's funeral, her mother was on the point of abruptly closing the door in her face, when Lucy intervened. She explained to her mother, that it might be good for her to have some company, someone to have a natter with over a cup of tea for a little while. Her mother acceded to her wish.

It was thus that a new friend was discovered and a new companion and partner in the fight against the wicked child sexual exploitation gangs, of whom there were now several up and down the country of many differing complexions, including the one in the City, whose criminal perpetrators were entirely of ethnic Pakistani background.

When Lucy and her visitor had sat down together in the front room, mother brought them both a cup of tea and biscuits and asked if they would like her to stay. Lucy responded that she need not remain as she knew how much work her mother had to do that day.

So in accord with her daughter's wish, her mother excused herself and the two sat down for coffee and to get to know each other.

So Lucy and Janice began a voyage of self-discovery and of a discovery of the other. They found that they had so much in common that Janice stayed until lunchtime and they found that they both had a central interest in closing down the brothel in the centre of town and freeing the girls, some of whom had already been imprisoned there for many years. They wanted also to bring to justice the local 'gangsters', who had set up the house of ill-repute.

The conversation was protracted and yet unfinished. They felt that they still had a lot to talk about. So they agreed to meet again the following day at a similar time. Janice promised that she would bring copies of her publications in local and national media about the issue with her for Lucy to peruse and keep, if she so wished.

So began a powerful new force in the fight to close not just one but all of the houses of child sexual exploitation across the country, liberate comfort and support the victims over a necessarily very long period of time and bring to justice the evil men who were organising the grooming and abuse of those young girls for financial gain.

Janice began by asking Lucy if Gran and she had already taken a look at the role of drugs in the grooming of young girls into sexual bondage.

"No, Gran and I had it in mind, but we never started it. But it was always an obvious factor in pulling these young girls into permanent sex slavery."

Janice responded positively suggesting that they have another look at it together.

"Well, let's just scan in our minds and on our computers the increasing impact of drugs and drug culture leading to addiction and the sort of sexual exploitation that is the central key to both of our preoccupations."

Lucy responded positively.

"Yes I agree. After all, it is the drugs side that appears to be the main but not exclusive recruiting instrument for the cases of the young white girls in some towns, perhaps in all urban areas. Often it seems to me that the drugs are used to induce co-operation and eventually absorption into the deviant sexual side. Drugs move from being a bribe to become a pay-back method for future services."

Janice added in amplification.

"We know that there are several major mafia organised crime group at the base of the drugs trade into the city, among them international ones like the Albanians and regional ones like the Liverpool group, from which the sex gangs can get the drugs they use to entice the young girls in the first instance."

Lucy qualified the point about the drugs lords by developing the ethnic dimensions.

"But where there are also, as in our City, social and patriarchal hierarchies based in concentrated majority ethnic neighbourhoods according to ethnic group appurtenance, it is no wonder that criminals from that neighbourhood set up ethnically unmixed gangster groups as the basis for their wicked activities. Nor is it surprising that such neighbourhoods, feeling threatened by the majority population in this their new country generate what are to us aberrant social groupings, clubs, associations, etc. to support their 'own' mobs and the criminal activities of those mobs."

"Yes, you're right!" Janice interposed zealously.

"These perfectly legitimate organisations are then often used as legal bases to engage in fighting for their own neighbourhood's criminals. By using inflammatory key words, such as racism or Islamophobia, they aim to support and defend their 'own' mobs from within these legal organisations. Thus seeking to legitimate the criminal activities of the mobs."

Lucy took up the word again.

"Yes! As in our own City the activists use those key words in their defence of their 'own', even if the people they are supporting are criminals and their criminal activities are abhorrent to the vast majority of that ethnic group."

Sadly, by that juncture it was lunch time and Lucy's mother invited Janice to stay and have a sandwich lunch with them. The invitation was snapped up and the lunch was brief so that they could continue their work into the afternoon. Mysteriously Lucy was beginning to banish her trauma.

Their combined work continued after the brief lunch pause as they began to explore the expanding dimension of sexual exploitation through social media platforms, which sometimes resulted in fatal results, the outcomes of which can be seen especially among young females.

Janice pointed to the power basis of such involvements.

"Sometimes referred to as sextortion, sexual domination and abuse can occur where the perpetrator has a privileged position over the exploited victim. For example this can be the case of a teacher, employer, radio, television or computer character or even a senior figure in a severely organised hierarchical family."

Lucy added another characteristic case.

"Yes, I agree and add to this the case of young girls being forced into marriage, sometimes to much older men, and of course the case of women being divorced by their husbands merely by dint of the man saying 'I divorce thee' three times in a Mosque. That is unfair and illegal in Britain and the women would be quite able under British Law to challenge the decision and claim damages from their former spouses. In the UK men and women are equal under the Law. But, usually unappreciated, such proceedings are also unfair to the children in such a divorce. They suffer too."

"Yes and such 'marriages' sometimes happen when the girls are at pre-puberty, sometimes as young as eight years old. That is most certainly illegal in this country. Additionally, there is the case of the older daughters, who much make a choice. Almost inevitably they seek the financial security of the father and continue to be used by the father almost as slaves to the father's wishes, sometimes into their late unmarriageable twenties."

Janice nodded in response and she resumed.

"It seems to me that sexploitation, as its sometimes referred to, can occur when any such an authority figure exercises his/her power position to manipulate the victim by threat, coercion, financial or other asset blackmail, structure of familial authority, threat of banishment from a family grouping, religion, etc. and force them to provide sex. With the number of social platforms available, evil men also extort sexually explicit visual material, subsequently using those materials to blackmail the victims for sex, money or to exploit the victims further."

Unfortunately at that point Janice jumped up in horror remembering that she had an important appointment upcoming shortly, a summons from her boss that afternoon concerning two of her reports.

"These are the two reports, which contained explicit reference to the social and ethnic appurtenance of the criminal gangs in this city, who are organising the grooming and seduction of the young girls and the ethnicity of the mobsters and neighbourhood population where the crimes were being committed."

She added apologetically.

"I'm sorry but I have this meeting with my boss at the Paper because he wishes to call me to account for using the very ethnic description we were talking about. The accusation is that the use of that description had opened the Paper up to very damaging accusations of Islamophobia and/or racism. So I shall have to break our discussion now, which I have enjoyed enormously. If I am still on the Paper after the meeting, I'll ring and let you know when we can next meet. Perhaps we could also schedule a couple of more active engagements with the relevant folk in the Police, Social services or NSPCC for live interviews with the staff concerned. So I must be off. Sorry."

Lucy was disappointed but wished her a safe journey.

"OK! Drive carefully and I look forward to our next meeting. Good luck with the interview!"

Lucy was clearly very sad to see Janice departing for what turned out to be a disciplinary hearing, whilst at the same time feeling enlightened by their meeting and all that she had learned that day and was planning for the next. She was whole-heartedly looking forward to working together into the future with her 'new Gran'. But the best made plans of mice and men ....

Chapter Thirteen: Delayed Success and Finale

Lucy watched and waited anxiously for the promised telephone call from Janice keen to learn what had happened in the disciplinary hearing, to which Janice was being subjected by the local Newspaper's senior management. She had little doubt that the charges against Janice would be summarily dismissed and labelled as an infringement of the basic right to free speech in a democratic society. Just a tiny worry maybe!

A positive outcome was important if the campaign to open up the can of worms that existed in the City and hopefully wider afield were to be successfully opened to Public knowledge. In that process she and Janice would be a vital and indispensable instrument in achieving that objective. Finally the telephone rang in the very late afternoon as darkness was beginning to fall.

The news was shattering and demoralising to Lucy. For her part Janice's voice was cracked with emotion as she shared with Lucy the news that she had been dismissed with immediate effect from her job as a senior reporter at the Newspaper.

Lucy began to offer her commiserations, but Janice cut her off, saying that she, Janice, needed to be alone and she would contact Lucy the following morning. The telephone went dead.

That was the last time Lucy spoke let alone saw Janice, although she did hear many years later that Janice had set up her very own successful Press Agency, through which she continued the campaign. She had married a fellow reporter on one of the national Newspapers, they had married and they now had three lovely daughters.

Many years later her disgraceful dismissal was rescinded and she was handsomely compensated. Eventually Janice's contribution to the dissolution of this nest of inhuman crime in the City was widely acknowledged and she was recognised and honoured by the City as well as nationally.

She was also called to give evidence at the much delayed trial of the gang boss, who after a very long trial, received a sentence of twenty-six years without remission at the Crown Court. While in prison, he was attacked on several occasions by fellow inmates and eventually died in prison.

The rest of the criminal gang were also arrested and tried and received sentences ranging from eight to nineteen years. Gran's murderer was sentenced to 30 years in prison. As one of the central organisers and perpetrators of the evil business, Yusuf was sentenced to 18 years but with the chance of remission, as he had pleaded guilty and acknowledged and deeply regretted the wickedness of his actions.

He was released half way through his sentence on the basis of good conduct and his services to his fellow inmates and their welfare during his own incarceration. On release he moved to one of the new towns in Durham and set up the plumbing business that he had always planned for when he left school all those years ago.

His company offered several apprenticeships every year including for girls and his business was said to be well regarded, cost-effective and reliable. He became deeply involved in a number of local childrens charities. He never married.

The Chief Constable, Sir Keith Bradley Jones and Mrs Sarah Wozny, Executive Head of the Local Authority Social Services and Youth Work Departments both resigned with Honour at the end of this torrid affair but left their marks on their organisations and the City to make sure that nothing like that which had happened in the past could ever happen again.

In both cases a regular examination was undertaken judged against the stipulations of the 2010 UK Equality Act, which sought to foster equality of opportunity and make it easier for people to understand their rights and how they could challenge discrimination.

The Law was aimed at protecting individuals from discrimination, harassment, and victimisation, based on nine protected characteristics: age, disability, gender reassignment, marriage and civil partnership, pregnancy and maternity, race, religion or belief, sex, and sexual orientation. It was well used.

As a result of the subsequent evaluation meetings to consider the Act and its implications for the Police Force, closer relationships with neighbourhoods containing large ethnic minorities were strengthened and enhanced and neighbourhood Policing was made more appropriate to the given neighbourhood.

A closer more interactive relationship was also developed between the two organisations, Police and Social Services with a more effective exchange of information between them and mutual staff exchange placements for short periods of time introduced and encouraged.

In the case of the Police, Community engagement was strengthened and joint and co-operative problem-solving with all local communities and partner organisations was strengthened. A major effort was also attempted to make the Force more community-sensitive and the number of School Liaison Officers was doubled.

With rising poverty in the city acknowledgement of the role of all religious communities in the provision locally and close to their house of worship of a multitude of services in the City, such as food banks and charitable home goods and clothing stores, meetings for different age-groups to counter loneliness, singing together sessions, and an additional host of mainly voluntarily provided charitable activities was highly praised in the City.

Sadly and more recently the Police Force had been hit with a multitude of allegations in the media and face-to-face of 'cultural appeasement' in the introduction of a preferential practice of discrimination against white job applicants and promotion decisions.

In the case of the Social Services, the focus on children and their welfare was strengthened as the central core of their work and there were no write-offs. For many years subsequent to 2010 the City's Social Services and Police had annually evaluated their performance against their co-operative criteria.

In both cases annual in-service development was introduced, however brief. Moreover, it was made incumbent on all employees to attend an annual evaluation and plan formulation for the succeeding year of professional development with their line manager. Once again, however, and sadly there had been a rising tide of allegations of preferential treatment for non-white job applicants and promotion seekers.

In the NHS too, there were widespread allegations of cultural appeasement with the NHS discriminating against white job applicants and favouring ethnic minorities. Fast-tracking the promotion of members of minority communities into senior jobs was alleged to be widespread in the service. The results of these policies have remained unevaluated.

With Gran gone and having lost the learning companionship of Janice, Lucy nonetheless found a spur for her academic studies. She ultimately left the College with three flying 'A' levels for a place at university, where she studied medicine.

She was lucky that her two main friends from College, Louise and Patricia, had also obtained places at the same university although in different subject areas. She made new friends as well and her continuing friendship with her existing friends from College meant that she had a wide and very satisfying circle of friends and a lively social life.

On successful completion of her studies she joined the staff of the local Hospital Trust, where she was eventually appointed as a senior haematology surgeon and contributed research into and the development of in-service professional provision in the field of sepsis.

She married a colleague at the hospital, had a family of two boys and two girls, who eventually all studied at the local College like several generations before them. She was well liked by colleagues at the local hospital and was deeply involved in the hospital's charities, especially the children's ones.

The Principal and Chair of the College Academic Board Mrs Sara Burnley Crowder, ultimately retired when she reached the age of sixty. She was immediately co-opted as a full member of the Governing Body by a unanimous vote of the Governors and allocated a special brief with regards to developments in Artificial Intelligence (AI) and its administrative and curricular implications for the College. She still had two of her grandchildren in the senior classes of the College and they were doing well and keeping clean!

In an attempt to improve their service both the Police and the Local Authorities drew fundamental conclusions from the criminal cases and the recommendations of the two major official reports, as well as the succeeding Equality Act and there were many changes in personnel, as well as organisational and procedural matters. Widespread alleged misogyny, fuelled by too many on-line bellwethers jousting for influence, in many of their institutions was addressed full-face on and several dismissals occurred.

The venerable NSPCC enhanced its honourable one hundred and fifty years record in the field of caring for children and was widely acclaimed to have gained in popularity for its sensitive yet responsive position throughout the crisis.

Sadly in a brightening picture almost universally, by the twenty twenties the pattern of child exploitation had spread nationally and the NHS nationally and locally was accused of having discriminated against white applicants for jobs in favour of ethnic minority applicants and of deliberately fast-tracking minority candidates in applications for promotion. Those debates still continue.

Acknowledgements

I am deeply indebted to my beloved wife, Margaret, for assistance with the titles and content of this modest Novella, for multiple proof-readings and for encouraging me in its final production. It could never have been achieved without her loving and enthusiastic support, as always in our sixty-seven years together.

I also owe a great debt of gratitude to our children, Mark, especially for the IT and Angela and Colette for their infinite understanding, support and assistance to me while I was writing this book in my dying days.

Especially as they have deeply influenced a number of the books I have written, I am beholden to my mother, Kate, and my father, Jimmy, for the tales they told myself and my brother, Brian, in the evening singing and story sessions at home, in front of the range fire, often in an atmosphere of quixotic flickering darkness. I should also mention the exchanges and lively singing the whole family engaged in with other working class families on Saturday evenings in the music room at what was universally referred to as the workingmen's club in the City's downtown Textile Hall.

Not least I am deeply indebted to the many accounts in several media and several official reports on the dreadful crimes, which I write about in this novel and particularly the Jay Report into Child Sexual Exploitation in Rotherham, which was so deeply thorough and influential and courageously began the process of tearing down the prejudice barriers behind the inaction of the authorities and the reactions of the community.

I also acknowledge a debt of knowledge to the report of the Independent Inquiry into Child Sexual Abuse that was established in 2015 and published several years later, some thirty and more years after the odious crimes concerned had first come to meagre Public attention.

Finally I should also like to acknowledge my debt to the mates, with whom I worked in the wool bins in the bowels of the beautiful Italianate textile mill near and across the river from the Moors, when I left school. In a similar vein, I am also deeply beholden to all the other colleagues from many different countries and hugely diverse backgrounds, with whom I have had the privilege of working over very many years and in many different parts of the world since my time in the textile mill wool bins.

Lastly I have to say that the lifelong and long ignored pain of the women and girls referred to in this Novella have made this the most difficult work of fiction that I have ever written. I offer my admiration and sincere congratulations that so many showed such immense and patient courage over so many years and eventually achieved justice of a sort. I admire them all dearly.

Works of Fiction by the Author

New Life in an Old Town: Part One of the Ayton Cycle (Available as e-book and paperback)

The Hydra (Available as e-book and paperback)

The Fit Country (Available as e-book and paperback)

Back-to-Back (Available as e-book and paperback)

The Final Mission (Available as e-book and paperback)

Turbulent Times: Growing up in the Edwardian Era (Available as e-book and paperback)

Deception: Part Two of the Ayton Cycle (Available as e-book and paperback)

A Boy's Story: A Novella (Available as e-book and paperback)

The Endless Struggle: Part Three of the Ayton Cycle (Available as e-book and paperback)

The Silent World (Available as e-book and in paperback format)

Armageddon: Part Four of the Ayton Cycle (Available as e-book and in paperback format in early 2024)

The House on the Blind Site (A book of short stories) Available as e-book and paperback in late 2024)

Travails of Youth: A Novella (Writing in progress for availability as e-book and paperback in mid-2025)

Unseen Community (Writing in progress for availability as e-book and paperback in late-2025 or early 2026)

Happy Poems and Games for Young Children (Complete but unpublished; awaiting a poetry editor and illustrator)

Other Books by the Author

Parents and Teachers, (with John Pimlott). Schools Council Research Studies, Macmillan

Multicultural Education, Routledge and Kegan Paul plc

Prejudice Reduction. Cassell

Change in Teacher Education, (Edited with Robin J. Alexander and Maurice Craft) Praeger

Education for Citizenship in a Multicultural Society, Cassell

A Human Rights Analysis. Cassell

Cultural Diversity and The Schools, (four volumes edited with Celia and Sohan Modgil), The Falmer Press

Policy and Practice in Lifelong Education, Nafferton Books

Education for Community, Macmillan Education

Education and Development: Tradition & Innovation, (four volumes edited with Celia and Sohan Modgil) Cassell

Multicultural Education in Western Societies, (With James A Banks), Holt Rinehart Education

Lifelong Education and the Preparation of Educational Personnel, UNESCO Institute

The Multicultural Curriculum, Batsford Academic and Educational Ltd

Education for Citizenship in a Multicultural Society, Cassell

Teacher Education and Cultural Change, (With H Dudley Plunkett), Linnet Books

Multicultural Education in a Global Society, Cassell

Provision for Children with Special Needs in the Asia Region, The World Bank

Reformkonzeptionen der Lehererbildung in Grossbritannien, Beltz

Lehrerbildung für den Unterricht behinderter Kinder in ausgewählten Ländern, (together with Professor Dr Wolfgang Mitter and Colleagues), Böhlau

Printed in Great Britain
by Amazon

61356705R00107